CAMP LAURA

CAMP LAURA

A NOVEL

PHIL MUTA

CHAPTER ONE

The main building was burned to the ground. Some charred wood scattered around the foundation was a small reminder of the great building that once stood there. All that was left was a portion of the brick chimney, still standing like a blackened monument amid the rubble. It was like looking at the tombstone of an old friend I had come to visit.

The main entrance was to the left of the building, and I parked my car in front of the chain across the gravel road.

"Dad, why did we stop here?" Mike asked.

"I just wanted to look around before we go back to Grandma's."

The kids and I got out of the car and walked over to the chain.

"Have you been here before, Dad?"

"Yes, Kim, a long time ago when I was around your age, well a year older. I used to work up here. I just wanted to see if it has changed much."

"Where did you work, Dad? All I see is a bunch of trees."

"Well, Mike, at one time there were lots of buildings around. See that building that burned down? That's where I worked when I was here."

"What did you do, Dad?"

1

"I worked in the kitchen. When everyone finished eating, busboys would bring the dishes back to us, and we would wash them. This place was once a summer camp with a lot of kids running around. I thought that all the buildings would still be standing, and it would still be a camp, but it's gone now. It looks like there hasn't been anyone here in a long time."

Kim and I stepped over the chain while Mike went under it. The main building was just to our right, and down the little hill to our left was the lake. The lake started almost at the road and extended to the woods about a half-mile away. Right behind the main building was another gravel road that led to the rest of the camp.

The kids wanted to see the lake, so we walked past the main building and down the hill slope to the lake.

Some of the lake was covered with algae due to years of neglect. A few decaying posts in the water were all that remained of the boathouse. The docks on the lake were gone, and the little beach was mostly dirt now. About thirty feet out from shore used to be a floating dock. It was there I learned to do my first somersault. Up and down that shore, kids swam and played. But that was long ago. Now only my two children were there to see how far they could skip a rock across the lake.

When I suggested we walk around some more, Kim and Mike asked to stay by the lake and throw more rocks. I could see they weren't too crazy about looking at some old buildings. "Okay, Kim, you keep your eye on Mike and be careful. Come back up to the car when you're ready to go," I said.

I went back up the hill and took the road behind the main building to walk through some more of the camp. I walked up to where the main building was. The dining area was mostly dirt now; there were bits of concrete slabs where the kitchen was. I can still imagine the controlled chaos we had during suppertime. Lats running around trying to fix everything, Clock trying to figure out what snacks he could bring down to our shack. Paul yelling at the busboys to do their jobs right, and Ed throwing the dishes that wouldn't come clean out the window into the lake. The five of us were just good friends; even to this day I still think of them as my best friends I ever had.

Walking back on the road, I could see where the tennis courts had been. Weeds and grass had all but taken over. Only a few barren patches of the courts remained. The fences around the courts were gone. This was the yard area where the campers and guests would sit around in the shade to visit and relax. The benches and loveseats were gone, of course. A few shade trees were left with their dead branches scattered among the weeds and bushes.

Further up, the gravel road separated the boys' and girls' cabins. What was left of the cabins was run down, most of the windows and doors gone. Her cabin was still standing, and I went in to look around. This was the first time I had been inside. Even after all these years, I still felt her presence here. I could picture her leaning out the back window, talking to me. Outside, the bushes and hedges around the cabins had once been trim and orderly. Now they were wild and unkempt. Past the cabins, the road curved and went up a small hill to the gym. At that curve, there was a path that went past her cabin, across the road and to our shack that we stayed in. The path was completely overgrown, but I could remember exactly where it was. Walking up to the gym, I could see that the farmer who probably owns the land now was using the gym as a barn. Once inside, I saw that the gym and stage were used to store hay. I walked downstairs to the canteen, but that was gone also. The booths and counters were replaced by old tires and farm equipment.

It was easy to picture the soda fountain counter and booths where they should have been. I could almost hear the jukebox playing. I wish I could see her again, waiting for me in the corner booth. I turned around and went back upstairs to the gym. When I got to the center of the gym, I took one last look at the stages. There used to be a piano there, and it was there that I fell in love with her. We spent a lot of our time sitting behind the piano trying to be alone. As I turned to leave, the sound of a piano playing stopped me. Of course, nothing was there. She was gone, and I would never be able to watch her play again. Wasn't it ironic that the last song she played for me on the piano was our song "As Time Goes By." For the moment, I swore I heard that song again. The wind blowing through this old building must have been making me imagine things. I had even thought I heard someone crying. We only had that one summer together. She was my first love and sometimes her memories keep coming back. Taking one last look around, I left the gym.

Standing outside the gym, I could look over most of the camp. It all seemed very sad. Maybe the main building being burned down was the way it should be. For us, the main building was the heart of the camp. With the heart gone, it looked like the rest of the camp had died, too.

Coming down the hill, I decided to go back to the highway by way of our old path. There were no remnants of a path now, but we had walked that path so much that summer, I could do it blindfolded.

The path took me behind the girls' cabins and down to the highway. Across the highway was the baseball field. The small stands and backstop were gone now, and the field was used as a pasture. A small dirt road separated the baseball field from the parking lot, which was directly across the highway from the main building. The lot had deteriorated to grass and bushes.

There used to be a fence that separated the shacks from the parking lot. The shacks were gone now. They were probably the first to go. I walked over to where our doorway would have been. I could still picture that plaque we had over our doorway. "Stalag 17." That was the name we had carved in it. Of course, the swamp in the back of our shack still remained.

I saw the "No Trespassing" signs posted on the trees that lined the highway. It didn't seem right. Behind those trees, kids ran, laughed, and played. They brought life to the land all around.

The sign was still standing at the main entrance, waiting for people to pass underneath it. But the only thing underneath it now was the chain and padlock. It had been a long, long time since it welcomed a guest. The sign was too old and weather-beaten to read, but I didn't need the words on the sign to remind me what it said. The sign once had bright blue lettering, "Camp Laura, Boys' and Girls' Camp," and it welcomed people to a place that was alive and happy.

It had been 20 years since that summer. I was struck with a feeling of loss and disappointment when I first saw the camp. I know I should have expected this, but I had hoped everything would be the same. Maybe I should have stayed away and just remembered it as it used to be. But although the years had taken their toll on the land, I realized now that the camp was not yet dead. The memories were all around, and each part of the camp brought them back. Those times had been some of the best of my youth. My mind went back to that time when this camp and its memories were a part of my life. Back then the time was simpler, and each day brought adventure and fun.

That summer, which seemed so long ago, had started as we finished our junior year of high school. It was the beginning of a long summer vacation.

CHAPTER TWO

Well, today was the day! Today I got up to make my mark upon the world. My first giant step to manhood.

"Philly, Philly, time to get up!" my mom shouted upstairs to me.

Christ, how am I going to go into manhood with a name like Philly?

"Okay, okay, for crying out loud, Mom, I'm up."

Getting out of bed, I looked over at my Casablanca poster of Humprey Bogart. Giving him a thumbs up, I said, "Here's looking at you, kid." I strive to be as cool as he was, so I could get a hot girl like Ingrid Bergen.

On my way to the bathroom, I stopped in front of the door mirror. What a sexy kid! Just think, I am almost 17 years old and a full-fledged man now. A little skinny, but with a little muscle there also. I went over to the door jam to check my height but I was at the same 5' 3" mark. When the hell am I going to grow? I haven't moved off that mark for months now. Another disappointment came when I still was unable to find a whisker. Damn, other kids my age have to shave a couple times a week. I can't even get one damn whisker. I don't even have hair on my chest. I bet my parents made a mistake on my birth certificate. I'm probably only 10 years old. That's why I am so small and look like a cue ball. I had taken my shower last night, so I just got dressed, and I was ready to go.

Downstairs my mom, dad, and older brother were sitting at the table eating breakfast. "Oh, my poor baby," my mom kept sobbing as she got up and went about getting my breakfast ready.

My mom was the typical Italian mother, a great Catholic, never missed church or bingo. We had a big crucifix of Jesus in our kitchen that my mom always talked to, mostly complaining about us boys. I kind of thought it was mostly about me. I was an altar boy in church, helping the priest during mass, and that made my mom think I should be a priest. She kept mentioning it to the cross, and I swear I think Jesus rolled his eyes every time. Mom had thick coal-black wavy hair without a single gray strand. She was proud of that. Mom thought that the only problem with the world was that people didn't eat enough. If all the world leaders would just sit down and eat together, there would be peace throughout the world. When one of us came home with a problem or there was the slightest sign that a germ had entered our body, the first thing Mom did was feed us. Her idea of a healthy person was one that eats all the time. Since I was small and skinny, my mom thought I was on death's door. She says it was those extra spoonfuls of food she talked me into eating that kept me alive.

Dad was doing what he always did. He just sat there drinking coffee and smoking. Later on in the day, the coffee would be replaced by beer. When Dad wasn't working, he was usually sitting at the kitchen table. This made it nice for us because he was never too busy to talk to us. Dad always let us do most of the talking, and no matter what we had to say, it would seem important to him, although I suspect he didn't hear a word we said. Dad was the tallest in the family. He had straight, thin hair and a slight beer belly. When he laughed, everyone on the block could hear him. We didn't have much, and people probably called us poor, but Dad still managed to bring little things like beer nuts or candy bars home for us. Sometimes he would sneak us down to the Carawana diner and buy us hamburgers with everything on them. And he would always tell us not to tell Mom, but somehow I think she always knew. Mom and Dad were okay.

My brother was a different story. We didn't get along, though we tolerated one another. To be "really" honest, my brother was a nice guy. Ask anyone on the street, and they would say he was a real cool guy. Ask any girl, and they would say he is a stud. That was the problem. My brother cheated me out of all the girls. If my brother weren't so greedy, I would have had girls all over me. I could have gone out with a different one every night. I could have gone parking, me and a couple of girls in the back seat. They'd be climbing all over my body. They'd be…Well, anyway, it was all his fault. Since he was the first one born, he took all the good stuff and left me what he didn't want. Talk about greed. My brother was average height. That he got from my dad. The thick wavy hair, he got from my mother. I was short. That I got from my mom. The thin straight hair, I got from my dad. I'll never forgive my brother for that. Every chance I got, I gave him the finger.

"Well, runt, you'll be home tonight," my big mouth brother said.

"Shut up, pea-brain," I answered as we exchanged our usual comments with brotherly love. "Mom, are you sure I'm 16? Could they have made a mistake at the hospital?"

"Don't be silly, of course you're 16. Why do you ask a question like that?"

"Never mind, Mom."

I didn't eat much for breakfast because I was anxious and excited. This was my first whole summer of work before I went off to save the world, and although I was excited, the fear of the unknown was beginning to take its toll.

As my mom went upstairs to pack some of my clothes, my dad was going through his coughing spell. My dad was a coal miner and a chain smoker, a bad combination. Every morning he would go through his coughing spells, trying to get his breath. Being a coal miner was all he knew, and he wouldn't give up the smokes. I waited for his coughing to slow down while he got another coffee and lit a cigarette.

"Son, don't get in the habit of drinking coffee. See how bad it makes me cough?" I waved the smoke away so I could get a clear look at my dad as I waited for his valued bits of wisdom.

"Well, son," my dad said between drags, "Behave yourself up at camp. You can come home any time you want. Just remember everything I told you, and you'll be okay." Dad always says that to me when he can't think of anything else to say.

My mom came downstairs with my clothes and was sobbing about her baby growing up, leaving home, and about how much she had sacrificed for us.

"Oh, Mom, cut it out. I'm only going for the summer," I said as I was getting anxious to leave now. Although my dad didn't say very much, Mom was forever making up for it.

Between the smoke and the sobbing, I heard a familiar low rumble increasing in volume to a medium-sized earthquake. I knew that my ride was here. Paul stopped his truck and blew his horn. It sounded like a constipated bullfrog.

I yelled out the door, "I'll be right out, Paul," as people were coming out on their porches to see what disaster had befallen them. I often wondered why the civil defense had not taken Paul's truck for a new early warning system.

My goodbyes were as expected. Dad was quiet but disturbed; while shaking his hand, I had bent his cigarette. Mom cried, and my brother gave me the finger.

I threw my bag of clothes in the back of Paul's truck and climbed in. Ed was back there and helped me up. Paul, Ed, Lats, Clock and I were friends that hung around together, and we all got jobs working together at this camp for the summer. Ed and I moved the tires, tools, papers boxes, and stuff that we had no idea what it was, to clear out a spot to sit down. We were careful not to dent or scratch "Sherman II," Paul's christened name for his truck. No one knew why Paul named his truck "Sherman II." I always wondered what happened to "Sherman I." We were also careful not to say 'truck' out loud, because Paul had an idea that Sherman had feelings, and he talked to it all the time. He would never admit how old Sherman was, a lady or a truck would never tell its age. Sherman was an old Ford pickup truck, mostly green with a red hood and yellow driver side door. Paul had added a wooden frame on the bed of the truck. There wasn't much on Sherman that was original equipment, for Paul patched it up with whatever he could find. I don't think Paul believed a muffler was a necessary piece of equipment on a truck. Sherman also had a tendency to tilt to one side because a spring was broken. It kind of looked like a truck with a hernia. To top off Sherman, Paul had added a railroad tie in place of the front bumper, "to give old Sherm some class," or so he said. Paul took criticism of Sherman as a reflection on him; he did the same with his truck, his girlfriend, and his friends.

Our next stop was to pick up Clock; in our group, he was the ornery one. To most of the girls, he was the cute, loveable, cool stud that they all wanted to hug and baby. Five or six of the girls on his street were there to see him off. Jeez, you'd think he was dying or something. Some of the girls were asking him to write and send post cards. Where the hell did they think he was going? China? Two of the girls hugged him, and they both kissed him real quick. He pulled away from them and climbed in the back with Ed and me.

"Clock, I hate you," I said.

Clock banged on the roof and yelled for Paul to take off. Paul in turn yelled at us to quit beating on Sherman.

Lats, the smart one, was the last to be picked up. The noise of Paul's truck brought some more neighbors out on their porches. As Lats was climbing into the cab, his parents were trying to calm them down. Hearing that we would be gone for the summer helped a lot. When everything settled down and Lats said goodbye to his parents, Ed, Clock, and I banged on the cab, yelling for Paul to take off.

"Quit beating on Sherman!" Paul screamed.

As we drove through town, we were hanging out the back, yelling our goodbyes to everyone we knew. Even people we didn't know were coming out on their porches to see us off, yelling something at us. The outpouring of love from the town was touching.

Driving away from town I thought, *Well, look out world. Here we come, ready or not.*

CHAPTER THREE

C amp Laura was about 4 miles from the Pennsylvania/New York State border. The trip up there was about 60 miles as the crow flies, unless the crow is drunk. It took us about 3 hours. The trip was uneventful except for the hitchhikers. We had to look twice to believe that they were girls. One was blond and short, usually the first thing I noticed in a girl, and the other one was medium height with brown hair. Both of them looked really good. But we were teenage sex maniacs; everything looked good to us. Paul finally stopped his truck when he got tired of us screaming and banging on his cab. As we backed up, the two girls were giving us some cautious looks. I was leaning over the tailgate, leering at them in what I considered my sexiest look. I think my tongue was touching the tailpipe. Paul was yelling at them to hop on. Lats was hanging out the cab window, telling us to act our age. And Ed was hanging on to Clock as Clock was trying to climb out the back of the truck to help them climb up. One girl looked at the other, and both of them took off running down the road away from us. I looked at Clock, who was looking kind of puzzled, and said, "Now what the hell did they do that for? I thought they wanted a ride." The rest of them were mumbling "Oh, hell" while

Lats was telling us how crude and uncivilized we were. Ed ended the debate with his unquestionable logic: "Girls, you can't figure them out. We can't live without them, and they can't shoot us," he said.

As we drove up to the camp, we noticed the lake on our left, then the main entrance with a big sign over it that said, "Camp Laura, Boys' and Girls' Camp." The first thing we could see inside the entrance was the main building. It was a large wood and brick building. It looked like the brick came up about four feet, and then it was finished off with wood siding the rest of the way. Paul told us that the big dining area was the section farther away, and the kitchen was in the middle. The other dining area was towards the road with the office off to one side. This was the guest dining room. A big fireplace was in the guest dining room. The roof was round like a big barn roof. Paul had worked at Camp Laura last summer as a dishwasher, and he was the one that got all of us jobs there this year. Just past the entrance he turned right and drove directly to our quarters. Across the road from the main entrance was a dirt parking lot and then a large 6' fence. Our quarters were behind that fence. Our home away from home was a 15' x 25' one-room shack. It was a small wooden building with a small front porch. It had a door, with windows on the other three sides. Except for the beds, it was bare with no heat and a light bulb hanging down in the middle of the room. Of course, to us this made it all the better, and we were unanimous in agreement that it was neat. There were 5 bunk beds in the place and no room for anything else.

I walked outside to look around; one look inside was all I needed. We had the end shack in a row of buildings. Our shack was next to a dirt road, and across the dirt road was a field which looked like it was also used for the camp to play baseball. Paul came out and explained to us that the building to our left was used to store junk. Next to that was a small building with two showers and two toilets for us, the hired help, and our laundry facilities. After that were two buildings that housed the laundry facilities for the camp. We were not allowed in those buildings. On our right was the dirt road separating us from the baseball field. Behind us was our own private swamp that I'm sure the owners wouldn't claim.

Back inside we set up the bunks, two on each side and one at the back wall. Paul had the first bunk to the left as we walked in. Paul was the oldest of the gang. He was 18 but in the same grade as the rest of us. Even though Paul was the biggest, strongest and oldest, he was just a teddy bear, a very big teddy bear. Paul was a big happy-go-lucky type of guy, who was about as strong as his truck. Everyone liked him. The few who didn't were scared into it. Paul weighed over 225 pounds and not one ounce of it was fat. He was about 6 feet tall and built stocky, with short hair that never saw a comb. His arm muscles were bigger than my leg muscles. Just one look at Paul told anyone he was not the type to mess around with. But what Paul looked like was altogether different from what he was. He had a great sense of humor with an ability for infinite patience. He needed it with us. Although Paul could probably have had his pick of any girl around, it would never have occurred to him to go out with any girl other than his girl back home. Joan and Paul could always be seen together and all the other girls were jealous as hell about that. Paul worked on his dad's farm most of his life, and sometimes Clock and I would help haying a couple of weeks in the summer. The younger and smaller ones like me would be on the wagon, stacking the bales. Paul was the only one who could throw two bales at a time. He was always sticking up for the underdog or the little guy, which is why Paul and I were such good friends. Because I was the best of both worlds, a little underdog.

The next bed on that side belonged to Ed. Ed was about as tall as Paul but was close to 75 pounds lighter. He had to anchor himself down when a strong wind came. Ed was the quiet one of the group. He went along with the rest of us in whatever we did. He did most of his talking around us. You really had to know him before he would open up. Ed kept everything pretty much to himself so he was hard to read. He was always there when we needed him, though. Ed was a good, dependable friend. A lot of people took his silence for being shy. He had a dry sense of humor, and he came up with some great one-liners. Ed was pretty sick as a kid, something to do with his heart, and his parents were a little over protective with him. They were always afraid he would get sick, and they didn't want him to do anything. If they knew all the stuff he got into with us, he would be grounded for life. When he hung around with us, he was one of the gang, and I think that is what he liked the best.

Lats took up the first bed on the right. Lats was a chunky guy who was always worried about something. He weighed a little more than Paul but was nowhere near as strong. He was always neatly dressed and well groomed. He seemed to say and do the right thing all the time. In other words, he was not like us in any way. You would think he would be smug and look down his nose at us, but he wasn't like that at all. He was our friend; we liked him and he liked us. Lats was the brains of the group. In fact, he was the smartest one in our class, also in the whole school. This made the rest of the kids label him as weird, which made him fit with our group perfectly. How he ever got mixed up with a bunch of misfits like us, I never knew. Ed and Lats were the best of friends; that was reason enough to be our friend. The teachers were always telling him not to hang around with us, like we were going to be a bad example to him. If you asked me, it was just the opposite; he was always trying to teach us those dumb things like logic and thinking. Lats was always against all of our ideas, but he always went along with them in the end. You might say that he was there to add some sanity to the group.

The next bed down from Lats was Clock's. Clock was about my closest friend. He was the joker of the group. He was the one who started trouble but always came out smelling like a rose. When we needed an idea, he always had one handy. Clock was fairly tall and husky. Although he wasn't as big and strong as Paul, he was pretty close to it. Clock had curly, light brown hair and dimples, with the impish face of a little kid who you just knew had the devil in him. He was always laughing and joking and clowning around. The girls went crazy over him. I guess he brought out the mother image in them. A couple of years ago we were playing baseball, and he broke his arm diving for a ball. Well, you would think that he only had a few days left to live. There were girls around him all the time, writing their names on his cast, they even carried his books for him and made all kinds of fuss over him. I'll tell you it was downright sickening. If he wasn't my friend, I would have puked. He was ornery and mischievous and always had his hand and nose in everything. Like Paul, he was intensely loyal to his friends, and we could always count on him.

Against the back wall was my bunk. My name is Phil, but only my parents and teachers called me that. I was known affectionately as "Kuni," pronounced as "could I." I really don't know where that nickname came from or who gave it to me, it just always seemed to be there. I was the littlest, weakest, dumbest and probably the most revolting one of the lot. My parents were the opposite of Ed's. I would leave the house in the morning and come home at night. They believed that if the bone wasn't sticking through the skin and I could stop the bleeding, I should be ok. Maybe that is why I was only 16 years old and on my second guardian angel. My first one probably had a nervous breakdown. For some reason I always wound up doing the dumbest things, with most of them close to illegal. I am pretty sure that put my mother's idea of priesthood for me out of reach. I was a good friend with everyone else there. I guess I was friends with mostly everyone in school. I was small and the girls called me cute and cuddly, but why didn't they want to baby me like they did Clock? Paul, Clock and I were the closest, but all five of us liked one another, and we all would stick up for each other through anything.

We put our suitcases under our beds and went up to the office to check in. The camp was a boys' and girls' camp with separate living quarters, of course. The office was in the main building that also housed the kitchen and the kids' and guests' dining rooms. It was a large, L-shaped building. It had the campers' dining room at the end nearest to the highway. The quests' dining room was at the other end. In the middle was the kitchen. The walkway through the kitchen had swinging doors at each end leading into the dining rooms. That walkway cut the kitchen in half. One side was the cooks' area and salad counters. On the other side were the dessert pantry and then our dishwashing area. It was kind of stuck in the corner. Off the guests' dining room was the office, which completed the letter L.

The camp was owned and operated by an old Jewish couple. It didn't take me long to figure out why it was a Jewish camp. The owners were Mr. and Mrs. Winderberg. He was a small man with a large nose and no voice. At least it seemed that way because he never said a word to us. He greeted us with a pleasant smile. He looked small and meek, and when I saw his wife, I understood why. She was a large woman who seemed to take up the whole room. She was tall and heavyset with the smallest feet and ankles I ever saw. When she talked, the room shook, and so did her husband. She said "hello" to each one of us and explained all the rules of the place, and there were quite a few of them. The rule she stressed the most was that we were not to mess around with any of the girls. I thought that if they all looked like her, that would be an easy rule to follow. We were also just the help and were not to mingle with the campers. She explained that most of the campers were rich, and some were snobbish and intolerant, so we were to keep to ourselves as much as possible. She did not like that behavior, but some of them were spoiled brats.

Ruth, as she wanted us to call her, didn't seem too bad, and I thought we might get along. They both seemed pleasant enough, not anything like I expected. She hugged Paul to welcome him back and greeted each one of us like we became part of her family. Mrs. Winderberg explained that we would be doing work around the camp for the first week. When the kids came in the next week, we would be full-time dishwashers. We would have a head dishwasher, who would be coming that next week. Paul already filled us in on that guy. Paul said that he was a mean, dirty old man that looked about 130 years old. None of us were looking forward to meeting him.

CHAPTER FOUR

After the introductions were over, Paul took us on a tour of the camp.

He started the tour in the kitchen where we were going to be working most of the time. He showed us the equipment we would be using when we got to wash dishes. After that Paul took us down to the basement. This was where the vegetable man worked. His job was preparing the vegetables for the cooks. Now and then it would be our job to help him unload the supplies.

We left the basement and went down to the lake. Paul pointed out the boathouse and docks. "This is where we will spend most of next week working," Paul said. "I think we will be painting the docks and getting the boats ready."

The boathouse was open on the lakeside where the boats just rowed in and docked. A short distance away were two docks used to tie up the boats being used. Out on the lake was a floating dock. Swimmers used that more than anything else. The camp had organized swimming periods for the campers, but we were allowed the use of the lake any other time.

We went back up towards the main building and turned left on a gravel road behind it. As we passed the tennis court and shuffleboard area, Paul said, "We are allowed to use these only when the campers or guests are busy somewhere else, which means just about never."

A little ways from there the road came to a 'Y.' Paul explained that the left fork led to the stables for the horses. This was also off limits to us. From there the riding and hiking paths continued into the woods. The right fork of the road led through the campers' areas. The boys' cabins were on one side of the road and the girls' on the other. This was also off limits to us, especially the girls' side.

The boys' cabins were arranged in a square with one side open and all the cabins facing the center area. It was a small area with a flagpole; it looked like some army barracks you see in the movies.

The girls' cabins on our right were the same except that they had a big fence and bushes growing around the back of the cabins. I wondered if it was to keep the boys out or the girls in. I'm sure that it wasn't meant to keep us out; we were such trustworthy boys, as close to sainthood as you can get. Passing the campers' cabins, the road curved left, taking us up a little hill to the gym. The entrance was at one end of the gym floor with a stage at the other end. The stage had curtains with a piano, drums, and a few other instruments on it. Paul said they put on plays and talent shows during the summer for the parents who come up for the weekends. We took the stairway to the left of the stage. That led us down to the canteen.

At the bottom of the stairway to our right was a soda fountain and counter with stools in the front. Booths lined the rest of the walls except on our left where double doors led to the outside. Right by the stairway was a jukebox. The campers like to listen to music and dance. The middle of the room was an open area for dancing.

Paul told us we could use the canteen in the evening after supper dishes were finished. He said this was the campers' favorite spot because they were pretty much on their own here.

As we walked down from the gym, Paul pointed out two large buildings to our left. "Those are the rooms for the guests. Ruth does not like to have anyone disturb the guests, so stay away from them," Paul said. A small parking area was just off the highway for their use.

When we came back to the curve, Paul took us along a path. The path wound through trees and bushes from the curve, behind the girls' cabins, and down to the highway. We came out across from the baseball field.

We crossed the highway and walked alongside the baseball field to the backstop. There a dirt road came down from the highway and continued on to down towards the pastures. This dirt road separated the baseball field from our shack. We walked past our shack to the laundry building and picked up our bedding.

The next hour we spent getting settled down. It could have been about 15 minutes if it weren't for the horsing around.

By his bed, Paul had one of those double picture frames that fold together. One picture was of Sherman II and the other of his girl, probably in order of importance. Paul was very loyal to Sherman and Joan; he loved them both. They were both jealous as hell.

Clock was spreading pennies on the floor around his bed. After he realized that we were staring at him, he explained that this was a good way to determine how he could trust his bunkmates, and besides, it was good luck. I told him he was nuts. Sometimes I wondered about Clock.

Lats was busy getting his hospital corners just right on his bed. He also had a little rack set up to hang his clothes and had everything else in order. Ed was still trying to figure out which way to face his bed. Me, I just threw a couple of sheets and a blanket on, and I was ready to go. I don't worry too much about details—I don't think we get along too well.

Clock called Lats over to help make a hospital corner on his bed. As soon as Lats's back was turned, I pulled one of his corners out. "All right, who did it?" Lats said as he came back.

"Paul did it," I answered. Paul started to chase me then, so I ran over and jumped on Lats' bed.

"Get off my bed!" Lats yelled.

Paul caught me and picked me up. "No, Paul, not my bed!" Too late, Paul threw me on Lats' bed, which gave the go ahead for Clock and Ed to jump on top of me. Paul decided to join in. Lats just shook his head in disgust as the four of us wrestled around on his bed. While we rolled around laughing and messing up Lats's bed, he kept telling us how childish and immature we were, so we grabbed him and threw him down on his bed and piled up on him. We all figured it was our job to teach him not to be such a tight ass.

After a while I asked Paul, "Where's that town you said was nearby?"

"If you guys are finished, we can take a ride over there," Paul said. As we left, I reached down and pulled the corner back out on Lats' bed.

Paul had told us of this town, "Deep Forge," down the road a couple of miles. He said we couldn't miss it.

We missed it. Well, actually, we didn't miss it. We just didn't look hard enough. We did see a sign, which said "Deep Forge, Pop. 127." What we didn't realize was that the other side of the sign said the same thing for people coming the other way.

On one side of the road was a grocery, hardware, feed store and gas station all in the same building. Across the street was a house with sort of a post office in the living room. Paul said that the rest of the town was farmhouses off on the dirt roads.

We took about half a minute out of our time to case the town and pick out our girl friends. As it turned out, there was only one girl around, and she worked at the general store. But we didn't mind because there was enough of her to go around. The rest of the guys decided that if she ever sat on my lap, I would disappear, so they left her for me. We got a couple of Cokes and gassed up Sherman II, and back to camp we went.

On Monday morning after breakfast, our first job was to visit the camp doctor. We were to get a little check-up. I guess they didn't want us to pass leprosy or something on to the campers.

The doctor used part of one of the guest buildings as a little hospital. He had his office, a couple of examination rooms, and some bedrooms for overnight patients.

But that's not all he had. He had a nurse. Not just any old nurse, but a nurse whose cup overfloweth. She was a big, tall blonde, a little younger than our mothers, though it would be awfully hard to picture her as a mother. If she were my mother, I would still be breastfeeding. The front of her uniform was unbuttoned to the point where they were just about ready to pop out. It seemed like that white uniform was stretched beyond its endurance, and when she stood up my brain went into shock.

"Clock," I whispered, "When I die, I want to come back as her uniform."

"Good morning, boys. I bet you're here for your examinations," She purred. "Please have a seat while I get some information from you."

"Boys," she said after a minute, "the chairs are right behind you."

The next thing I knew Lats was pulling on me and Clock, trying to guide us to the chairs.

"What? Oh, sure," I said as I backed up to the chair and fell over the coffee table. That seemed to bring me back to reality. I scrambled up to a chair. She just shook her head, smiled, and asked our names and other information about us.

It was Ed's turn first, and his head kept bouncing up and down as she spoke. He was having a hard time. Every time he spoke, his voice broke. You could tell he was answering in pain. Ed told her all of his childhood ailments, which she was interested in. She sure asked him a lot of questions.

Clock kept repeating himself when it was his turn. He really got flustered when he said he had a pair of tits removed, then tried to explain that he meant tonsils. We all informed her that he had his brain removed also.

When she came to me, I almost forgot my name. She was rattling off questions to me, but I was lost in fantasyland. "Are you sure you are answering these questions correctly?" she said as she bent down to meet my eyes.

"What?" I said, snapping my head back. "Oh, sure that's right. Why?"

"Because you answered 'yes' to having a heavy menstrual period," she answered sweetly.

Oh, God! I thought as I slowly slid down in my chair. That stupid Clock didn't help matters when he fell out of his chair laughing.

After all the questions were over, she got up and led us to another room. That had to be a sight to see: a beautiful nurse leading five sex-crazy, drooling teenagers down the hall. Little did she know that we would have followed her anywhere. She put us in a room and told us the doctor would be in to check us out.

"Oh, my God, what a set of lungs," I said when she left. We all started laughing because we all let out a sigh of relief at the same time.

The doctor came in to examine us. He was tall and skinny with horn-rimmed glasses. He had a slight accent when he spoke. The examination was okay except we all got embarrassed when we had to drop our pants and cough.

When we finished dressing, the nurse came in with some small bottles. She handed them to us and told us she needed a urine sample. Lats and I were the first to go to the bathroom to fill our cups. We turned our backs to one another and started to fill the bottles. As my bottle filled up I found out I couldn't stop. *Oh shit*, I thought. *Why me?* I hurried over to the toilet as fast as one could hurry with his pants down by his ankles. By the time I got there, I had overflowed the bottle and got my hand and the bottle all wet.

How could you do this, you blockhead? I kept repeating to myself as I finished. By this time Lats had already left, and Clock and Ed were coming in. I shook my hand and pulled up my pants to leave. I walked up to the nurse to try to explain what happened, but she just reached over and took the bottle from me. Boy, if looks can kill, I would have died right then. She stood there holding this wet bottle not saying a word; I think she was counting to 10. She put the bottle down and took me over to the sink to wash my hands. While I was washing my hands, I was trying to explain, but she didn't want to hear a word from me. I was so embarrassed. I looked for a crack in the floor to crawl into.

"Boy! I never want to go through that again," I said to the guys as we went back to our shack.

Clock said, "Kuni, you are a lying sack of shit. You loved every second of it…even though you did piss all over your hand."

"Clock, I hate you."

The rest of the week we worked our butts off getting the camp ready for those brats. We were up at 5:30 and ate at 6:00. Boy, breakfast was out of this world—none of us ate that good at home. The cooks gave us all we could eat, and for growing teenage boys, that was a lot. There were pancakes and eggs, ham, or bacon at every breakfast. Potatoes or sausage and gravy were thrown in about three times a week. We ate like kings—well, maybe more like pigs—every morning. Paul told us to enjoy it while we could because once the campers came, we would never see ham, bacon, and sausage again.

After we did the breakfast dishes, we worked around the camp until noon. We ate, did the noon dishes, and then worked around the camp until supper. After supper dishes, we dragged ourselves down to the bunk and were too tired to horse around. The only break in the week came when Lats talked me into going down by the docks to get 10 feet of shoreline from one of the guys working on the boathouse. He claimed he wanted it to tie down something in the laundry. I spent about an hour looking for that shore line, until someone asked me what I was doing, and when I told him what I was looking for, it dawned on me what an idiot I was by the amazed look on his face.

During lunch they kidded me about that. "Hey, Kuni, are you going to look for a sky hook this afternoon?" Paul asked.

"Oh, screw you!" was my snappy comeback.

"Boy, you sure were dumb," Clock said.

"Oh, yeah!" I replied. "Well, I couldn't have been that dumb because it took me only an hour to figure out how dumb I was."

"What do you mean?" Lats asked with a puzzled look on his face.

"Well, Lats, if I was real dumb, I would still be looking for it." I answered and left. Lats never could follow anything illogical as he sat there trying to figure that out.

All in all, we were pretty anxious for those kids to get here so we could just worry about washing dishes. This other work was killing me.

CHAPTER FIVE

Throughout the weekend, the campers arrived with their parents. Some of the parents probably had second thoughts about bringing their children up to this camp. As they drove into the parking lot, they saw five weird-looking kids standing on a broken-down truck, sizing up their little darlings. As each one came in, we had a comment, like "Hey, look at the body on that one," or "That one looks like a fruit." I had noticed that they all came in fancy new cars and were dressed up. Paul had told us that all the kids came from rich families, and some of them were nice, but some were snobs.

On Sunday afternoon, our head dishwasher arrived in camp. Paul introduced him as "Joe," but as we got to know him better, we affectionately started calling him "Joe the Slop." I had my first look at a dirty old man. Joe was around 60 years old but looked like he was 90. He weighed about 80 pounds and was even shorter than I was, if you can believe that. There were only three teeth in his mouth, and his face was wrinkled and dirty. You could smell him 10 feet away. He had a sneer to go along with the rest of the image.

Joe took us aside and asked if we had any girl friends and if we could fix him up with one. I immediately started trying to think of someone I really hated, but found out I couldn't hate anyone that bad. After telling us a few dirty jokes, which embarrassed us all, he left for his bunk. He had his own shack on the other side of the laundry building, and we were glad it was a lot farther than 10 feet away.

"What the hell was that?" I asked as we got back in our shack.

"Boy, he's a regular sweetheart," Clock said.

"We had a lot of trouble with him last year." Paul replied. "The guy is as crazy as a loon. I can't understand why they let him come back this year."

On Monday morning, we started our first day as official dishwashers. Our work area was like a big U. On the back corner of the kitchen was our dishwashing machine. At the end of the machine was the outside wall with a window to let the steam out. An open stainless steel counter went all the way around except along the back wall where the dishwashing machine was. At the open end was the silverware machine where I was assigned to work.

The busboys brought in the dirty dishes and set them on the counter. Joe, our resident dirty old man, was the slopper. This was the job assigned to the head dishwasher, and it paid the most. It was also the dirtiest job, but Joe seemed to fit right in. The counter to Joe's right had two holes where two garbage cans were placed. Joe would take the dishes and scrape the foodstuff in one garbage can and papers in the other. He passed the silverware down to me to be washed. Paul was at the side next to the wall. He would take the dishes Joe had scraped and put them in a rack. When Paul had a rack filled, he would start the dishwashing machine and send the rack through. Clock took the rack as it came out and unloaded it. Ed and Lats would then put the dishes away.

By the second day, we had a routine well worked out. We would head up to the kitchen about 5:45 A.M. for our breakfast. Getting our breakfast from the cooks, we would take it to a table in the campers' dining room. Around 6:30, Joe the Slop would come in to sit by himself and drink coffee. Boy, I never saw anyone look as mean as he did in the morning. After we were finished, we went to our work area and got ready. The campers came in to eat about 7 A.M. and just about the time the dishes started coming in to us, Joe would come back and put his apron on. Checking the garbage cans, he would make sure he had plenty of room left in them. The dirty dishes would start coming in about 7:30, and we were usually finished about 9 A.M. when Joe would have Paul drag out the garbage pail for the maintenance men. The food scraps were given to a farmer for his pigs. The other garbage can Joe would fix by stomping down the paper. That can usually lasted all day long, and at night one of us would take it out to burn.

From 9 to 11 A.M. was free time for us. At 11 A.M., we went up to the dining room for lunch. The campers started eating at noon. We were generally finished with dishes by 1:30 P.M. and had free time till 5:30. Supper for the campers started at 6:30 and by 8 P.M., we were finished for the day.

By the end of the first two days, Joe had fired all of us at least once and a couple of us twice. Ruth told us not to worry about this as he did it all year last year. So we just kept working. But needless to say, Joe was getting under our skin.

The first week was about all we could take. Joe would come in after breakfast and start yelling at everyone. Paul was doing more and more of Joe's work, and Joe was getting meaner every day.

Breakfast was the only time all of the help ate together. Since we were such a pleasant and refined group, we began to make friends fast. After all, who could resist a bunch of sweet kids like us?

Most of the other workers were bright-eyed and raring to go. But our gang looked like death warmed over. Paul looked like some nightmare that would wake you up, shaking with terror. Ed looked like the headless horseman with his head still on. Clock's hair looked like he stuck a fork in an outlet. (Wait a minute. His hair always looked that way.) Lats looked like he was going on a job interview, spit and polish. Me, I looked like they not only hit me with an ugly stick, but beat the hell out of me with it. Mornings were not our best side.

The first person to be noticed by us was Alice. She was a chambermaid, along with her mother. They remembered Paul and came over to introduce themselves to the rest of us. There were two other older chambermaids like Alice's mother, but they kept to themselves, and saying "Good morning" was the extent of our friendship there. Alice's mother's name was Bernice, and she was very nice. Bernice was in her middle fifties with her short hair turning gray. She looked at least a couple inches taller than me and sat straight and precise in her chair. Pretty soon Alice and her mom ate with us in the morning. Bea, as we started calling her, gradually became our mother away from home.

Now, Alice was like her mother, and we all liked her. She acted just like her mom– pleasant, shy, and quiet–but boy, the rest of her was something else. Alice was as tall as her mother and had short hair like her, but her face was clear and had a shine to it. Her eyes seemed to sparkle. The uniforms they wore were about as plain as you could get in clothes, but she still managed to look sexy with them. Alice always smelled like she just took a shower with ivory soap. She was beautiful, and we all fell a little in love with her. It seemed that Lats had the best chance with her, and he sure wasn't wasting any time. The fact that her mother liked Lats best didn't hurt any. Clock could have had a little chance, but by this time he had his eye on a camper by the name of Jean. Paul had his eyes only for his girl back home. Ed was still bored by it all, and I had my eye out for anything that moved and was female.

The next one we became friends with was the third chef. His job, I guess, was to help the other two chefs. His name was Jimmy Prince, and he was the first black man I met up close. He would always be singing and telling us stories. His dream was to make it big as a singer. He was in his fifties, but I guess a dream is a dream no matter what age you are.

The second chef was a younger guy named Todd. He was friendly and seemed like a nice kid. We were his food taster group. He would bring over some of his cooking for us to sample, but little did he know that we were pigs and everything tasted good to us. The main chef was an older man who was full of himself. He was always putting down everyone else in the kitchen except us. We were beneath his station, we were the dishwashers, the lowest level of kitchen help. As far as he was concerned, we didn't exist. The top chef was the only one who was a real chef, the other two were in training.

The baker was an older woman, probably in her 40s. I think she had a crush on Clock or thought he was her child, because she gave him a lot of mistakes to take back to the shack for us. Paul said she was just a nice lady.

At the end of the first week, I declared war on our head dishwasher. Now, I already had the impression he didn't care too much for me, but when he started throwing silverware at me, my suspicions grew. I set my brain to work to devise some way to get back at Joe. Of course, the rest of the guys all had their own ideas, but I wanted this to come from me only. I hurried up with my lunch and got finished first so I could put my plan into action. While everyone else was still eating, I went to our area and got the garbage pail for papers and filled it 2/3 full of water. I loaded the rest of it with paper. All that was left was to sit back and let nature take its course. As Joe and the rest of the guys came in, I started to get to work to appear busy.

"You bastard, I told you to dump this can last night!" Joe yelled as he saw the garbage pail filled with paper.

"Okay, I'll take it out now." I said.

"Never mind now, you little bastard!" Joe screamed, as he stuck his foot in the can to stamp down the paper. His foot went down to the bottom and there he was, one foot in the can with water up above his knee and hate in his eyes. As we all started laughing, he came charging out of that can cursing me with stuff I never, ever, heard before. Paul stepped between him and me, and it caused him to come to a quick halt. He was so mad he was stuttering his swear words at me.

The next day, Joe spent the morning swearing at me until finally Paul told Joe to keep his mouth shut. That kept Joe quiet, but I found myself doing all the dirty jobs for breakfast and lunch dishes.

After the lunch dishes were done, Ed came over to Clock and I. "How would you guys like to watch some tennis?"

"I was thinking of going swimming." I answered.

"Well I bet I can change your mind. I want to show you something first," Ed said as he led us over to a window in the guests' dining room. "Who do you see on the tennis court?"

"Ed, you just changed my mind." I answered. Clock was already halfway out the door when we caught up to him.

"Okay," Clock said, "Let's not make this too obvious."

We tried to appear nonchalant as we watched the nurse play tennis. That is to say, we tried. Watching her bounce up and down around the court was just about all we could stand. She had a short tennis outfit on, and it looked like she grew into it when she was ten.

We watched her for about 5 minutes before I realized someone else was on the court with her. He was a counselor, 19 or 20 years old. He looked like a football player with muscles bulging out all over the place. This guy was taller than Paul and looked like he was posing for a muscle magazine. Paul doesn't look like Mr. America, he just looks like a big mean truck.

After the game they politely congratulated each other, trying to appear completely casual. But they were bumping into one another a little too much, and he quite accidentally happened to pat her on the behind. Casual, my ass, we were beginning to realize there was something going on there. Some younger boys started goofing around on court, and Mr. America came back on to give them some lessons.

We watched the nurse towel herself while she was watching this guy teach these kids for a while. Damn lucky towel. She wrote something on a piece of paper, and he came over to where she was. She passed that note to him when she shook his hand saying goodbye. While he toweled himself, he read the note and casually walked over to the garbage can. He must have ripped it up because he dropped some pieces in the can.

Ed, Clock and I played some shuffleboard as we waited for them to get finished and go back to their cabins. Finally, after what seemed like an hour, they left. When we were sure they were going, it was a mad rush to that garbage can.

For how long it took us to piece that note together, it wasn't worth it. All it had to say was "Tonight."

"What do you make out of that?" I asked Clock.

"It looks like she is going to meet him somewhere tonight," Clock answered. "They must have already lined up a spot."

"I wish I knew where, I would love to be there when they meet," I stated.

"Wherever they are going will have to be after dark," Ed said. "I think we should arrange to be by the doctor's office about then."

Clock and I looked at Ed, and I said, "Ed, you're a genius. Between you and Clock, I can always count on a completely corrupt and evil idea."

That night we rushed through the supper dishes in no time. By this time, Lats guessed we were up to something. He just knew coming from us it would be illegal, immoral, illegitimate and in bad taste. Lats didn't have a high regard for our ideas, which is the reason we wouldn't tell him what it was.

"Paul," Lats said, "they are up to something. You better go with them."

"I'm going to write a letter tonight. Besides, it's your turn to watch them," Paul replied.

"I wouldn't be a party to anything they cook up. I don't even want to know what it is," Lats answered.

Later on that night three strange kids were hiding in the bushes watching the guests' building where the nurse's quarters were. Finally, when it was almost dark, she came out. She looked like she was just taking a casual walk but, ha, we knew better. Trying to look as disinterested as we could, we followed her.

She led us around the camp for a while and finally settled at the boathouse. When she got to the door, she looked around to see if it was clear. Ed ran into a tree as we made a mad scramble for cover. After she ducked in the boathouse, we settled down to wait. Sure enough, about 15 minutes later, our Mr. America came by. Checking first to see if it was clear, he ducked in the boathouse. Ten minutes later we crept closer. Not hearing anything, we softly went around to the far end of the boathouse by the window. There we could hear some moving around and heavy breathing. Eventually our moaning and heavy breathing was almost as loud as theirs, so we had to get the hell out of there.

"Oh, my God! I couldn't take any more of that," I said as we got safely away. "I was becoming more excited than they were."

While Clock and Ed were commenting on that, a germ of an idea started to spread in my warped mind. *No*, I thought to myself, *I can't be that rotten. Oh, what the hell, sure I can.* Then I thought that Clock and Ed would never go along with it. After all, I'm the only one that would be mean enough to do something like that. Even though they would reject the idea at once, I decided to tell them anyway.

"Kuni, you're crazy!" Ed stated.

"Yes I am."

"I love it, what a great idea!" Clock said.

"Kuni, there is hope for you after all," Ed stated. With that, we finalized our plans.

The first thing we did in the morning was to find out the nurse's name was Olga. The next thing was for me to have a talk with Joe the Slop.

"Joe, I didn't know you knew Olga," I said.

"Olga, who the hell is she?" he answered.

"The nurse, you mean you didn't know her name?"

"Oh, her, why?" he asked. It looked like he was foaming at the mouth as he said it.

"Well, when I was talking to her she asked about you a couple times," I said and left to let him mull over that.

Later on at lunch, Clock and Ed were alone with Joe and happened to steer the conversation around to the nurse.

"Boy, that Kuni is lucky. I sure wish she was friends with me," Ed sighed.

Joe brightened up. "You mean that little bastard knows her?"

"Oh yeah," Clock added. "They know each other real well. She went with Kuni's uncle for a long time. She was almost part of the family."

Joe cornered me the first time he had the chance. "What did you mean she was asking about me?"

"Well, she just wanted to know your name. She said something about you being cute to cuddle."

"You better put in a good word for me," he growled at me.

"I don't know. She's my friend and even though she likes older men, you're a little too old for her."

"Look, you little bastard, if you want to get on my good side, you better fix me up for a little action with her."

"Well, Joe, I'll see what I can do."

With that out of the way Clock, Ed and I kept our vigil at the tennis court. For three days, we watched. Lats kept trying to convince Paul that we were up to something real bad; he could just feel it. Meanwhile I kept making up all sorts of stories to stall Joe, but I was running out of them. Finally, our watching paid off. Olga came to play tennis with Mr. America. After he gave lessons to the kids, they got on court. I wish we could have gotten closer, but we didn't want them to notice us. When they finished their game, they talked and appeared to agree on something. That was it. Our plan would go into effect tonight.

We got Jimmy Prince, the cook, to write a love note for us. When I gave the note to Joe, I swear a leer spread over his face.

The note read like this:

"Joe, you interest me. I like mature men and I think you could teach me everything I want to know. Please meet me in the boathouse after dark tonight. Be very quiet when you come in. I will be ready and waiting for my first lesson. I hope you will be ready also."

I was really proud of that note. I figured that should stir up the old letch, as if he needed anything to stir him up.

After dishes we went to our hiding place by the boathouse. It was just getting dark when Olga came along, followed shortly by Mr. America. About 20 minutes later Joe the Slop came. He was already starting to get undressed as he quietly slipped in the door. We in turn slipped on down and locked the door. It didn't take long.

The first thing we heard was a muffled scream.

"Who the hell are you?" Mr. America yelled. "What the hell are you doing here?"

Someone was rattling the door trying to get out. Mr. America turned on the lights inside.

"Who the hell is this old man?" he asked Olga. "And why the hell doesn't he have any pants on? Who the hell are you?" he kept on saying.

We heard more clawing at the door, and then Mr. America started chasing Joe around. We heard the pitter-patter of bare feet until Joe finally got smart. He ran towards the boats and jumped in the lake. He swam out of there faster than I've ever seen an old man swim. When he got to shore, he took off running up the road with his bare behind shining in the moonlight.

Olga and Mr. America came swimming out of the boat-house, and off they went up the hill. We could still hear him as they went out of sight.

"Who the hell was that old man?"

I was laughing so much that tears were coming down. When our laughing and rolling around the bushes had tapered down some, we got up to unlock the door.

"I didn't know Joe could swim that good," I said.

"He didn't have anything like a bathing suit to slow him down," Ed answered.

"Just a second," Clock remarked as he ran into the boathouse.

After a few minutes Clock came back out all smiles. "We're not finished with the job," Clock said and held out Joe's pants.

"Are you crazy? I'm not going to be the one to give him back those. He'll kill me," I told Clock.

"Who said anything about giving them back?" Clock grinned.

"Where can we put them?" Ed asked.

"I know just the place," Clock answered. "We need someone who can shinny up a pole."

"What the hell are you two looking at me for?" I said. "Clock, whatever you're up to, I'm not going to do it."

How the hell did I get talked into this? I thought halfway up the pole.

The next morning at breakfast the campers were all trying to find out whose pants were hanging from the flagpole.

Joe the Slop had his heart set on killing me, but Paul stepped in and told him to leave me alone.

By the end of the week, Joe had packed and left. I never could find out if he was fired or quit. The boss would not offer any explanation, only the fact that Joe was gone. Paul knew but he would not tell any of us.

Paul was made head dishwasher to the relief of all, especially the girls. He took his place as the slopper, and everything started working smoothly. Life began to settle down, and it seemed that we'd been there for years.

CHAPTER SIX

After working on the job for a couple weeks, we developed a good routine. As we cut down our time to do the job, the boss cut down on our help. Lats was the first to be taken from our dishwashing crew. His new job was to assist the salad chef. He cleaned and cut up the vegetables for the salads. When the pantry-aid man quit, Clock was next to go. His gift of gab was considered wasted on dishwashing. His new job was to help the pantry chef.

Even though there was just Paul, Ed and I washing dishes, we still cut down on our time. When I was caught up with the silverware, I would move over and help Paul slop and rack. Ed would unrack and stack the dishes to be put away whenever spare time was available. If we still had some dishes stacked when Lats and Clock were finished, they would come over and help us put them away. No one left until we were all done. With Paul as our head dishwasher, we were able to work better and faster, much to the delight of our bosses.

So now with this extra time, we decided to expand our social life, which would not be too hard since we didn't have one to start with. I just had to do something other than drool over that nurse all the time. It was beginning to have an unhealthy effect on me.

Lats was getting along pretty well with Alice, and it looked like something was cooking there. Clock was getting the hots more and more for this camper named Jean. But so far Clock couldn't even get the stove lit, much less get anything cooking. This was a shock to all of us—we had never seen Clock strike out like this before. The rest of us weren't in the running for anything. Most of the time we went for a swim in the afternoon and a shower at night. After our showers, we would horse around in our shack or go up to the canteen to drink cokes and listen to records. Of course our main purpose was to look at the girls. You could tell by now that all this excitement was almost more than we could bear. We were going like a herd of turtles. Our routine was definitely going to change.

Across the border in New York was a little diner called "My Place." It was a kid's hangout with some pinball machines, a pool table, and a jukebox in the back room from the eating area. This was where some of the local crowd hung out. Paul had been up there a couple times last year and told us all about it.

Paul also said they had some easy girls there. Well, Paul didn't really say 'easy.' I think 'nice' was the word he used. At this stage for us 'easy' was a hell of a lot better than 'nice.'

So that night Lats and Clock came over to help with the dishes and by 8:30, we were out of there. After showers and getting dressed, we were at 'My Place' by 9:30.

After getting a coke, we watched a couple kids play pool. Some girls were looking our way with interest and the local boys were not too happy about it. Lats was getting nervous over it all. Clock, Ed, and Paul could care less that the local boys were unhappy. I was more interested in the pool game.

I have a hard time passing up a pool table; I've played pool ever since I was able to see over the table. I may not be able to do many things right, but I can play pool with the best of them.

A couple of girls got brave enough and came over to talk to us. One of them was really laying it on thick for Ed. And Ed, not being one to miss a trick, welcomed it. They wanted to know where we were from and how long we were staying and so on. The other girl made the rounds first to Paul, then Clock and Lats. She didn't make too much headway with them so she settled on me. She was small and had black hair cut short, not too pretty but what the hell neither was I. When I'm around girls, I try not to say too much because I get nervous and say and do dumb things. So I bring out my alter ego, Humprey Bogart, and I impress them with my super coolness.

"Of all the gin mills in the world," I said, "you had to walk into my place."

"What the hell does that mean?" she answered.

"Nevermind," I said, "it was a different time, it was a different place."

She sighed and asked, "Why do I always get stuck with the weird ones?" and she walked away.

Not everyone understands my super coolness.

About that time a couple busboys from camp came in with three girls. When they saw Paul, they came over and sat in the booth next to us. It looked like they were glad to see some friendly faces. The busboys usually don't have anything to do with us, but we were the only friendly faces there. Besides, it is always better to let everyone know that Paul was your friend.

As we were passing out the hellos, it was my chance to notice the girls with them. That girl that Clock likes, Jean, was one of them. She was a real pretty girl, and it was easy to see why Clock liked her. She had long black hair with a little button nose and very sexy lips. Another one of the girls was a tall, well-built girl, but it was the extra girl who was just tagging along with the other four that caught my interest. She looked two inches shorter than me with long brown hair tied in a ponytail. I'm only sixteen, but she looked like a kid to me. That is, until I really noticed her face. She had a really cute face, but somehow it looked older than the rest of her. The thing that stood out the most was her glasses. It looked like she was wearing the bottom of two coke bottles. She was smiling, but to me it seemed like she was forcing it. I thought I could see a sadness in her face. I don't know why, but I had this urge to go over and hug her. Most of the other four did the talking, while she just sat there. I couldn't seem to take my eyes off her. Listening to them talk I found out that her name was Naomi, and she was best friends with Jean, who Clock was moving in on. She wasn't talking too much, but to me she stood out the most. Everyone else kinda faded in the background. This was really a strange feeling for me.

What broke the spell was when six or seven guys from around the pool table drifted over to our booth. I guess they were trying to intimidate us. We weren't too impressed. With Paul and Clock around, it's pretty hard to scare us. When that failed, they went back to their pool table to try another approach.

One of the kids that hung around the pool table was of special interest to me. Every place with a pool table has a top player; I've been in enough pool halls to spot them. This kid was the top dog here. You can watch these ringers, as I call them, but you only see how good they can be when it's a money game. It just seemed that he would be really good. I wanted to play him because I always figured I was pretty good also. By the way they were talking to this kid, I had a feeling I was going to play him real soon.

Lats, Clock and Paul were talking to those people from camp. Meanwhile Ed was busy at the jukebox with that local girl.

"Clock," I said when I had a chance to break in, "it looks like we're being set up with a ringer."

"Who is he?" Clock asked.

"That tall guy with the light blue shirt."

"Do you think you can play him?" Paul asked.

"I guess so," I answered.

The kids from camp wanted to know what was going on, and Paul explained that they were going to try to set us up with a pool shark. It's a pecking order to show us who the top dog is.

"What they don't know is we have one, too," Paul said.

A couple guys from around the pool table came over to us and said, "Are you guys up for some pool action or do you just sit and drink cokes?"

The guy that spoke was the bigmouth that was trying to scare us earlier. He must be the chief tough guy in town. As Bigmouth spoke, Ed started over to our booth. From the way he was making out with that local girl, I'd say Ed was getting all the action he wanted.

"What kind of action are you talking about?" Paul asked.

With the preliminaries out of the way, they began to get serious. At first Paul suggested he play Bigmouth. But

Bigmouth came up with some excuse and suggested Paul play the ringer. Well, Paul asked around the rest of us and with the usual excuses, it was decided I play the ringer. It would be a straight game of 50 for twenty dollars.

"Well, Kuni, get over there and beat his ass," Clock said, as we all put in our five dollars.

"Good luck," the girl with the coke bottle glasses said as I got up to play.

"Thanks. How could I lose now?" I answered. Something great happened then—she smiled at me. After that smile, I wasn't going to let anybody beat me.

Everyone gathered around the table to watch us play. We flipped a coin and I got stuck breaking first. I could have done without that. I hate being the first to break because for me it is a disadvantage. Trying to make it seem like I muffed the shot, I hit it so it would miss altogether and come up from behind to hit the rack. I heard some snickering and laughing as I stepped back to let their ringer shoot.

He looked at me for a moment and said, "I might be getting more than I bargained for."

"Two can play the same game," I answered.

He then went right out to get me. I had hit the rack a little too hard, and he was able to put a ball in. He ran the whole rack and most of the second one. There was some good shooting he did, and he played like he didn't want to give me another shot. By the time he missed, almost everyone in the place figured I lost. That is, everyone that didn't know me. Clock, Ed and Paul had seen me shoot before, and they weren't worried. Lats, on the other hand, had never seen me shot and had already kissed his five dollars goodbye.

I finished off the remaining balls and ran the next rack just to show him I could do it also. By this time everyone knew they were watching a good pool game. We weren't fooling anyone now. We were just trying to make the best shots we could. He had me 43 to 36 when he messed up. He was down to the last ball on the table, and it was at one end of the table with the cue ball at the other end. When the balls were racked up they were placed between his cue ball and the ball he had left.

He knew it was a hard shot so he played it safe and kept the cue ball up on the high side of the table. I still had the rest of the balls in my way and couldn't let him have another try. I called a cushion shot in the corner pocket. What I had to do was bounce the cue ball off the cushion to get around the rack of balls, and then I had to hit the ball and knock it into the corner pocket. That is, if my prayers were loud enough to be heard.

I took my time studying that shot. He was surprised that I was going for it. I guess he thought I should play it safe too. When I hit the cue ball, I knew it was going to be a good shot. It banked the way it should and hit the ball just right. Everyone held their breath as the ball rolled into the corner pocket. I knew the game was over with that shot, and so did he. I had left myself with a good combination shot off the racked balls and from there I finished the game. I took the twenty dollars and went over to the guy I was playing. We shook hands, and I told him he was a hell of a good player. He said his name was Tom and that I played a hell of a game. I bought him a coke and told him to call me Kuni. Well, Tom seemed like a nice guy, but the rest of them weren't.

Bigmouth went outside and a couple other guys went out with him. They stood out there milling around, I guess waiting for us. Tom told me to watch it because they were going to start a fight. It seemed that it was their money I had won. Paul didn't seem too worried about it, but the campers were worried enough for all of us.

"It looks like they are trying to pick a fight," one of the campers said. I think they were getting a little scared.

"Naw," I said, "They just want to welcome us to their friendly town. I think they must be the welcome wagon of the town."

Finally, when Paul finished his drink he got up and said, "Let's not keep them waiting," and the five of us walked out.

They were standing by their car, and when we came out, they dared us to come over there. Well, we didn't need a bird to crap on our heads to know a fight was in order. We bunched up and strolled over. As we stood and listened to Bigmouth's taunts, Paul moved in on him, right in the middle of his threats, where he was telling us how he was going to wipe up the street with us if we ever came back. Paul wasn't much of a talker; he just punched him square in the mouth. Blood came squirting out of his nose and mouth. He went rolling down the side of the car till he ran out of the car to hold him up. He hit the ground hard and stayed there. After Paul hit him another kid jumped at Paul and ran right into Clock's fist. Paul turned to the rest of the guys and nobody moved. I could imagine what the rest of them thought, for when I saw Paul hit him, I figured if that was me he would have taken my head right off.

"Let's try to cool down a little here," Lats said as he tried to settle things down, "We don't want any trouble. We came up wanting to be friends."

"Hey," Tom said as he came over and put his arm on my shoulder, "let me buy you a coke now. Maybe we could play another game, but this time no money bets. Okay?"

Tom and I started back to the diner and everyone started drifting back with us.

Paul then went over to help Bigmouth up. The kid was crying, and he jumped in his car and drove off. I guess the idea of mopping up the streets with us lost its appeal. Clock helped the other guy up, and he seemed to want to forget the whole thing.

For the rest of the summer we didn't have any trouble with them. We heard later that Paul had broken the kid's jaw. I guess that had a lot to do with our good relations at the place from then on.

The next day at the camp the fight built up to a riot, and we became instant heroes. Well, at least Paul and Clock became heroes. Even I received a little notoriety from my pool game.

CHAPTER SEVEN

Ed, Clock and I were back at "My Place" a couple days later, with Ed making up to that same local girl from the other night and me playing pool with Tom. It seems like he was the only one who wanted to play me.

That other local girl, the short one with the black hair, was there also. She kept hanging around smiling and talking to me. She was making me so nervous I couldn't play worth a damn. Tom beat me two out of three games of eight ball.

As we were getting ready to leave, Ed asked me if I wanted to double date Friday night. Now I may be a klutz when it comes to girls, but that doesn't make me want to take up being a priest unless priesthood went co-ed. I jumped at the chance and said yes before he got finished.

On the way back I asked Ed what we were going to do Friday night. "I don't know," Ed said, "Joan just said they will come by to pick us up at 8. I guess we'll do a drive-in or something."

"Hell, Ed, I don't even know what her name is."

"Don't worry. Her name is Cathy and she thinks you're cute. She said she had never been out with anyone as shy as you. I think she wants to take your cherry away from you."

"I don't know Ed, I spent a lot of time preserving it. It's a pickled cherry by now."

By the time Friday got here I was scared stiff. During the breakfast dishes Ed came over and asked if anything was wrong.

"No, Why?" I answered.

"Because that is the third time you washed that same load of silverware."

"What the hell is the matter with him?" Paul wanted to know.

"Kuni is going to lose his cherry tonight," Ed answered.

"Screw you," was my snappy comeback as I started the machine again.

"Will you stop washing that load of silverware?" Paul yelled as he came over and shut the machine off.

Lunch dishes didn't go any better, and by the time supper dishes were done, everyone in the kitchen was fed up with me.

After we showered, Ed and I waited while everyone else sat around and made cracks about me losing my virginity. Finally Joan pulled up in a two-door, light green Ford. As we walked over to the car, Cathy pushed the front seat up and got in the back seat. Well, I guess I'm supposed to sit there too, I thought to myself. I'll just sit down next to her, real cool like. She must have thought I was going to sit on my side cause she moved over to get closer and I sat on top of her.

"I'm sorry." I said as I jumped off her and then bumped heads with Joan as she was moving over to let Ed drive. I started apologizing to Joan as Cathy pulled me down next to her. Geez, I bet Bogart never did anything like that.

Driving back into New York, Joan leaned over and said something in Ed's ear. When we got to a store Ed stopped and went in. Pretty soon he came back out with a couple of six packs. When we parked at the drive-in, the girls excused themselves and went to the ladies room.

"Christ, Ed, I think they want to get us drunk. I always thought it was supposed to be the other way around. This girl is out of my class. She probably knows more than I'll ever learn. What the hell am I supposed to do if she wants to go all the way?"

"Take it easy, Kuni. It won't get that far on the first day. I hope."

"Hope! Hell, Ed, I don't have any protection. What happens if she gets pregnant? Oh, my God, what happens if I don't do it right? Maybe I might get lucky and drop dead before the movie is over."

"Here they come, Kuni. Dummy up."

"Boy, dummy is right."

The girls came back to the car laughing and giggling about something. Joan passed a couple cans of beer back to me. I opened them up and gave one to Cathy. We sat back to watch the movie and drank our beer. By the time we were on the second can, we didn't even care that the movie hadn't started yet. When the movie finally started, we were necking hot and heavy. We were just kissing but compared to my other experiences with a girl, that was hot and heavy.

Boy, if we keep this up, I thought, *she could get me drunk and have her way with me.*

The beer started having its effect and I was getting braver. I even started to unbutton buttons. *Hell, there ain't nothing to this.*

When they left to go to the bathroom again, Ed asked, "How are you doing back there?"

"Hey man, I got this all down pat. If I knew it was this much fun, I would have started when I was six."

After the girls got back they asked if we wanted to stay and see the rest of the picture or if we wanted to leave. "See the rest of the picture? What picture? I haven't seen the beginning yet," I answered, which goes to show you how much I was enjoying the movie.

The girls suggested we go somewhere and just talk. Following Joan's directions, we wound up parked on some dirt road leading into a pasture. Cathy was keeping her distance, and I couldn't understand what I did wrong. Pretty soon Joan suggested to Ed that they go for a walk and let us work out our problems. They got a blanket out of the trunk and off they went.

As I turned around to say something to Cathy she grabbed hold of my neck and pulled me down with her. We started making out like crazy and this time I got to those important buttons and undid them. That was the first time I ever saw a bare one in real life. She had to tell me to quit staring. A little while later we were both in stages of undress. I was getting my pants down, thinking, *Oh boy, I'll be a man tomorrow. God I hope I know what I'm doing and do it right.*

Just about that time a big, bright light started shining in the car. I jumped up and saw a tractor coming up the pasture. Cathy yelled, "A farmer is coming! Do something!"

"Hey, what the hell are you kids doing here?" the farmer was yelling out.

I started climbing over the seat while I was trying to get

my pants back on at the same time. I fell over the seat and my back landed on the horn.

"Get off the damn horn, and let's get the hell out of here," Cathy said.

With my back laying on the horn and my legs hanging over the seat, what the hell did she think I was trying to do? As I struggled to reach my shorts and pants that stupid horn kept blowing, along with Cathy yelling at me to stop blowing the horn. Finally I rolled off the steering wheel and fell to the floor. My face was on the gas pedal with my feet on the roof. And in between, my bare butt was sticking out there for the entire world to see. *Oh God, why me. I don't ever remember seeing Bogart doing something like this; how the hell do I get myself into all these messes? How am I going to explain this to Bogart? I am going to get kicked out of his cool club. This is going to be in our yearbook, under most likely to fail in a triple x movie. I am never going to live this down.*

I pushed myself out of there and finally pulled my pants up. Joan and Ed came running over as I started the car. The car was already moving when they jumped in the back seat.

"What the hell is with you and that horn?" Ed asked.

"Ed, don't go there. It wasn't pretty, and you don't want to know."

Cathy climbed over the seat to join me, and the girls were gabbing about a mile a minute. Cathy was telling Joan about my little bout with the horn and my pants. As she was explaining it, Joan and Ed kept laughing more and more. It sure didn't seem that funny to me. The girls decided that they had had enough excitement for the night and brought us home.

"Ed, if you say one word about tonight to the guys I'll kill you."

"Hey, you guys," Ed said, as we walked in the door, "guess what happened to Kuni tonight?" Ed started giving everyone a vivid account of everything that happened. It started with the guys laughing, and then it went to down right hysterics.

"I hate you guys," I said, "it's not that funny, it could have happened to anyone."

"No, Kuni, you're the only person in the whole world that would have happened to," Clock answered, "and you still have your virginity."

"At least I'm not the only virgin here." I stated. I looked at all the guys and there was dead silence. "Oh my God, I am the only virgin here, Ed, Lats, please tell me I am not the only virgin." Still dead silence.

"Kuni," Paul told me, "it's no big deal, don't worry about it."

"Hell, at the rate I'm going, my tombstone is going to read: He died the worst of deaths, he died a virgin."

"It will come," Paul answered, "and when it comes, I hope love is involved."

"Kuni," Clock said, "we are all jealous of Paul, we all want a girlfriend like Joan. When you do lose your virginity I hope it's to a girl like Joan."

"You know, maybe I don't hate you guys after all."

"Well what are you going to do when you lose your cherry," Clock asked, "take out an ad in the paper?"

"I don't know, maybe I'll go to the Virgin Islands and get recycled. I do know that I get scared shitless thinking about it."

"No one here will admit it but we were all scared, the pressure to do it right and not disappoint her makes us all scared," Lats said.

"Yeah," Ed added, "when Kuni loses his cherry, we should all go out and get drunk, hell, it should be declared a federal holiday. They had one for Washington when he cut down a cherry tree. Kuni losing his is a hell of a lot more important."

"Ed," Lats injected, "the holiday was not for cutting down the cherry tree."

"Lats," Paul said, "don't stop him now he's on a roll."

"We could celebrate by ringing bells shaped like little cherries and setting off cherry bomb firecrackers," Ed continued.

"Have a cherry picking contest. The one that gets the most cherries wins," Clock added, "It could be called Kuni's lost cherry day."

"No, I was wrong. I do hate you guys."

CHAPTER EIGHT

Now it is usually our nature to get along with everyone; at least that is our opinion. Sometimes in nature a storm comes up. Well, storm clouds were brewing with us now. We were becoming increasingly annoyed with our co-workers, the busboys.

The busboys were campers who worked in the kitchen during the meals. They worked for extra spending money and to supplement the cost of camp. It was their job to serve the food and to gather up the dirty dishes when the kids were done. They would put the dishes on carts and bring them back to us. After the busboys unloaded the dishes on our counters, we would wash them. The busboys were treated on the same level as counselors and had more privileges than the rest of the campers. This put them at a higher class than us. We were the workers, there to work for them, but it didn't bother us at all. We looked at it as a job like any other job, and we got paid for it. This didn't sit well with them. Some of them thought we should consider ourselves beneath them. Well, that was never going to happen.

Now we have a hard time trying to think of ourselves as lower than someone else. Maybe a little dumber and poorer, but never lower. We were having a hard time swallowing their attitude.

At first, we didn't say too much, thinking their noses would come down a few notches as time went on. It appeared, after a while, it was just getting worse.

Those busboys were mostly from larger cities. They didn't realize that us kids from the coal mining area of northeast Pennsylvania are not to be looked down upon. Of course, some of us you have to look down on. In my case just about everyone has to look down at me. But in general the kids from our area are not to be trifled with, 'cause they make them big, hard and wide in PA. The busboys' day of reckoning came when they trifled with Paul, the biggest, hardest, and widest of the lot.

The breaking point came on a day when it seemed like everyone was finished eating at the same time. The busboys were bringing the dirty dishes faster than Paul could slop and rack them. The counter was getting filled, and the dishes were stacking up. When one of us gets piled up, someone will go over and help, so I slipped over to help Paul.

In every group there is a loudmouth. I should know cause I'm the loudmouth in our group. The busboys had theirs, a kid named Harry. Harry must have figured he was pretty smart or we were pretty stupid. He always had some sly remarks to say. Most of the time I never knew what he meant, but it always sounded like a wisecrack. Harry was unloading his bus as Paul was dumping the slop in the garbage can. It was a large twenty-gallon can and about half full then.

Harry looked at the can and said to me, "Instead of giving that can to the pigs, I think I'll suggest to the boss they feed it to you guys. It's not good enough for pigs."

Paul reached across the counter and grabbed Harry by the shirt and lifted him right over that counter knocking dishes all over the place. When Harry's feet cleared the counter, Paul set him down into the slop can. With Harry standing in the can up to his knees in slop, Paul said, "Now it's good enough for pigs."

Even though that incident caused us some problems with our boss, the problems with our busboys came to a screeching halt. The idea of Paul reaching over the counter and picking up Harry, who was a pretty good-sized kid, and pulling him over the counter kind of put a damper on their attitude. Their attitude probably didn't change much, but at least they kept it to themselves. As for our trouble with Ruth, our boss, we were ordered to a command performance in her office. She sat there and listened to our side of the story. Although she may look like a stormtrooper, she is pretty nice and also understanding. She did not like the way the busboys were treating us at all, and she apologized to us about it. As we left, however, she informed us that we couldn't go around sticking her campers in garbage cans. We were to refrain from doing it again.

We soon got our routine down pat and started to work on our well being, so with Clock in the pantry and Lats in the salad department, we soon began to stock up on our food supply. Clock's job was dishing out dessert and sometimes if it was good, whatever was left found its way to our shack. Most of the time we were in awe of Clock's ability to scrounge stuff. I think he could be put in the middle of a desert with nothing and a week later you could find him in an oasis with 5 or 6 Arab women waiting on his every need. Have I mentioned that I hate Clock?

As we were finishing up the noon dishes, Clock came over and told us to meet him by the basement door.

Clock was up to something. Lats started saying that he didn't want anything to do with whatever it was. When Clock is up to something, somewhere along the way there's trouble.

That noon we had watermelon for dessert, and sure enough, when we got down to the basement there was Clock sitting there with two big watermelons and that stupid grin on his face. He also had about two dozen bottles of soda and four bags of chips.

"We're going to have a party," Clock said. "Jean said she would stop by our shack this afternoon and bring some friends if they can sneak on down there."

Ed and I gathered around Clock and praised him for his natural ability at being a crook. We drooled over the loot while Clock explained to us how he got all of it. Meanwhile Lats nervously paced the basement floor, just knowing the boss was going to come in any second. About the only thing Lats agreed with was Clock being a good crook.

"You guys went too far this time. Someone is going to see us with all this," Lats kept saying.

"Don't worry Lats," Ed said, "I'm sure they will put us all in the same cell."

"Well, now that you got the stuff, what are you going to do with it? We can't stay here forever," Paul finally said.

Paul did bring out one good point. How were we going to get it to our shack? We would have to take the stuff across the road and through the parking lot. The whole trip would be in plain view of the camp.

"Most of the campers are back in their cabins getting ready for the afternoon activities so there shouldn't be too many people outside," Clock said. Before we could think of any objections, Clock said, "Okay, let's all grab something and stick it under our shirts. No one will notice us."

We all went over to get something to carry. By the time I could get in there I was stuck with a big watermelon. As everyone started out, I sat there trying to figure out how the hell I was going to get that watermelon under my shirt and down to the shack. I finally said the hell with it and wrestled it under my t-shirt. Maybe I would just look like a fat kid. But as with all great crimes, there were a few things that didn't go right.

For starters the watermelon was almost as big as I was. Another thing was that my t-shirt only covered the top half of the watermelon. I started my journey bent over carrying the stupid thing and waddling up the road like a dumb duck. With my luck, when I got to the road, three cars had to be going by. Boy, I got some strange looks from those cars. *Yeah, Clock*, I thought, *no one will notice, no problem. Clock I hate you*, I said to myself as I waddled across the street and started down the parking lot. The rest of the gang was already at the shack watching me and cheering me on. Feeling proud of myself, I started to waddle faster and dropped the stupid watermelon. I looked down at the rest of the guys as they all scattered. The watermelon just laid at my feet split in two. I felt like I was in front of class in school giving a speech with no clothes on. Stupid Clock.

"Okay," I said to myself, "I've got to remain cool and calm. Don't panic." So I picked up the pieces of watermelon and ran like hell.

When I got down to the shack, I gave the watermelon to Clock and told him where he could stick it. Since I had watermelon all over my pants, shirt and me, I decided I better take a shower and change clothes. I grabbed a towel and went over to the shower.

I wasn't going to put those sticky clothes back on so when I finished I just wrapped the towel around me and went back to the shack. When I walked in everyone just stopped talking and looked up at me. Jean and two other girls were there.

The girls started giggling and I looked at everyone and said, "Towel, don't fail me now. Clock, could you get me a shirt and pants out from under my bed? I don't think this would be a good time to bend down and get them."

At that the girls broke up completely. Taking my clothes from Clock, I backed out and got out of there as fast as I could. *For christ's sake*, I thought, *timing sure isn't one of my better qualities.* Getting dressed, I debated about waiting out here till everyone left, but I figured I had better take my medicine and go back in there.

"Hello everyone," I said as I stuck my head in the door. "You probably don't recognize me with my clothes on, but I was here earlier." That got the girls laughing and giggling some more as I came in. Why do girls giggle so much? I sat down and eventually everyone got back the subject they were on when I so rudely interrupted.

I sat over by the door drinking some soda and eating chips, hoping no one would notice me again. One of the girls with Jean was Coke-Eyes; at least that is how I remembered her from the diner. Her glasses were still about a half-inch thick. Well, she came over and sat by me, and I froze. I stupidly shoved some chips at her, trying to pick some words out of my brain to say.

"Hi," I said. *God is that the only one I can come up with?*

"Hi. You know you are about the best pool player I ever saw," she answered as I stared at her.

"I just got lucky. He was a good pool player."

"I bet you don't remember me, do you?" she said again.

"Let's see now," I started. "You wore your hair in a ponytail with a light blue ribbon in it. You were wearing jeans, blue, with a light blue top, drinking a cherry coke and looking at your watch a lot because you wanted to go home. Jean told you something funny, and you tipped your head sideways to your right and laughed, and it brightened up the whole room. I liked that. I thought your lipstick was too bright and you had a sad look on your face that night, and you were forcing yourself to smile most of the night. I thought you had the cutest little nose I've seen. You looked at me when I got up to play pool, and you said good luck and smiled at me. I think I could have beaten anyone in the world after that. No, I don't think I remember you. Were you there?"

She just looked at me for a minute, stunned, and said, "That's amazing. My name is Naomi. What's yours?"

"Phil, but everyone calls me Kuni."

"Kuni, what a strange name. How did you get that nickname?"

"It's a weird story. Are you sure you want to hear it?"

"Yes."

"Well I was out walking in the woods one day and I came upon a bush. All at once a bolt of lighting came out of the sky and struck that bush. It burst into flames and from the sky a loud booming voice spoke. "Hark young man, from this day forward you will be known as Kuni. Go forth and spread your wisdom throughout the lands. Enlighten the masses with your charm and wit."

"You're nuts!"

"Yes I am," I answered.

She laughed and punched me in the shoulder. "No seriously, how did you get it?"

"I don't know. It just seemed like I always had it. But weren't you impressed more with the other story?"

"You're silly. Yes, I was very impressed, but more by what you said earlier."

"What were you and the rest of the campers doing up the soda joint in New York ? Of all the soda joints in the world, you had to pick my soda joint."

"Well, I needed to hear Sam play our song one more time. Really we heard about it, and Jean drug me up there with her. Boy, we were sure glad to see you guys when we came in. That place was a little scary."

"I see you know about Rick and Sam also. It sure is nice to meet a girl that is as crazy as me."

"You guys didn't seem scared at all," Naomi said.

"The place wasn't too bad. After our ability to talk and reason with them paid off, they have been friendly ever since."

"Is that what you call talking and reasoning? It sure seemed like a fight to me."

"No, everything went fine once we found the right words to use."

"You guys are crazy. Do you get in trouble like that often?"

"No, how could such nice, loveable guys like us get in trouble? Besides, most people don't mess with Paul or Clock," I answered. "I know sometimes Paul can be scary, and Clock isn't afraid of anything, but the both of them are just two big teddy bears."

"I think Jean likes Clock. What is he like?"

"Well, Clock and Paul are my best friends, so I might be a little biased. Clock is one of the good guys. He would always be there if any of us needed help. If we need a hand up, a kind word, a laugh, Clock will be there to give it. I think Clock can find something happy and fun out of the worst time. Jean couldn't find a better person to like."

"And what about you?" Naomi asked.

"I'm just another kid, shorter than most, nothing special."

"Well," Naomi answered, "I think you're funny and weird. You are very easy to talk to and you made me smile and laugh. I haven't done much of that lately, I would say that makes you very special."

We sat there and continued to talk until they had to go. Boy, I didn't want them to go. Well, I really wanted her to stay, but everyone else could have left.

After they left I sat down on my bed and wondered why the hell I told her that goofy story about Kuni? Why the hell do I act so stupid around girls? For once, I wish I could be cool, like Bogart or Cagney. Instead, I act like Laurel and Hardy.

CHAPTER NINE

Lats was out on a date with Alice tonight, and we knew he would be coming in late. We all figured he would be tired when he got back, so keeping with our image of being just a great bunch of guys, we decided to fix up his bed for him. Clock thought it would be a nice gesture to remake Lats' bed. But instead of laying the sheet all the way down he folded it back up to make it appear like two sheets. For the people who don't know, this is what we call short sheeting a bed. It works great for tall kids, but Clock tried it on me once, and I slept in it all night and never knew.

We heard Alice's car drive up, and we shut the light off and jumped in our beds to pretend we were asleep. Lats came in and got dressed for bed, pulled back the sheet and jumped in. We heard a ripping sound and then quiet. After about three minutes, we heard Lats call over, "Ok Clock, what the hell did you do to my bed this time?"

Paul got up, turned the light on, and there laid Lats with his legs sticking through two holes in the sheet. Needless to say it took us quite a while to stop laughing. Meanwhile Lats just lay there saying over and over "I'll get you for this, Clock, I'll get you for this."

After everyone settled down and we all fell asleep, I woke up in the middle of the night. I slid out of bed and went over to Lats' bed, "Lats, do you want to get even with Clock?"

"What do you have in mind?' Lats answered.

"Follow me!" I said. We quietly went over to the shower building, and I had Lats fill up a pail with some water. "Ok Lats, when we get back I want you to lift up Clock's hand and place it in this bucket."

"Why do you want me to…Oh I see now. Kuni, that is sick."

"Yeah, it is, isn't it?" I said.

We got back to the shack, and Lats quietly went over and placed the bucket of water by Clock's bed and placed his hand in it. The next morning when we got up Clock had already broken down his bed and had his sheets rolled up for the laundry.

"Lats, I know you couldn't have come up with that by yourself," Clock said while he was looking at me.

"Thanks," Lats said as we walked up to the main building for breakfast.

That night Jean had agreed to meet Clock up at the canteen. Lats was going somewhere with Alice. And Paul was staying in to write some letters. So Ed and I took Paul's truck and went up to "My Place" to hopefully meet some girls.

After scouting around the place for about a half hour, Ed locked into a couple of girls sitting in a booth by themselves. They were sitting there alone since we came in so we figured they were waiting to meet two handsome devils like us. Since we didn't want them to suffer any longer, we moved in.

Ed started putting on the charm, or laying down the bull-shit, depending on how you look at it, and it looked like he hit pay dirt with one of them. Now my charm isn't anywhere close to Ed's, and when I try to lay down bullshit, I usually wind up sitting in it. So I let Ed do all the talking and like my idol Bogart, I just stood there trying to look cool, dashing, and debonair. I think the other girl thought I was deaf and dumb.

They were both sitting on one side, so I slid in the booth on the other side with Ed following. We started with small talk to break the ice. While we were getting to know one another, I mentioned my name and they wanted to know if I was the Kuni that went out with Cathy. When I said yes, they whispered to one another and got into a hysterical giggling fit. I just sat there getting redder and wondering just what the hell that girl told them.

Judy was the girl Ed was trying to hit on, and Carol was the one left for me to try for. I was trying out my best Bogart on Carol, figuring who could resist that? When she got out a pack of cigarettes for a smoke, I knew this was a golden opportunity for me to show what a really cool guy I was. I saw Bogart light a cigarette and then hand it over to the woman so if he does it, what can go wrong?

I reached over and took the pack from her, saying "Here let me do that for you." I tapped the pack against my finger to pop out a cigarette. After I put back the five extras that came out, I put one in my mouth and tried to light it with my famous one-hand match-lighting technique. I broke the first match, burnt my thumb with the second one, then gave that up and lit the third one the regular way.

Lighting the cigarette, I coughed and said, "I usually can light the match the first time, you know I smoke quite a bit myself, I started when I was a kid."

"You're lighting it on the wrong end," she said.

I looked down and saw the filter burning. "Oh!" I exclaimed as I went to take it out of my mouth. My mouth was dry so the cigarette stuck to my lip, causing my fingers to slide down the cigarette and burning them on the filter. As I cried out in pain, I got mad and tore the cigarette out of my mouth taking half of my lip with it. Overcome with pain, I dropped the cigarette in her coke.

I took another cigarette out, and this time I lit it right. I gave her the cigarette and smiled as my lip was bleeding profusely. She looked at the cigarette with my blood on the end of it and said that she changed her mind. She said she decided to quit smoking and drinking Cokes.

Ed and the other girl got up to dance, so not to be out done, I asked Carol to dance. She was silent for what seemed like a long time, but then said, "What the hell."

We both slid out of the booth, and I turned to take her hand. I grabbed her knee by mistake. My god, I thought, as my eyes followed her standing up. This girl is tall, not just tall for me, but tall by any standard. The valley between her breasts was eye level for me. Any other time that would have been just fine for me, but getting ready to dance didn't seem like the best time for this to happen. For Christ sake, if that's not bad enough I also realized that I don't have the slightest idea how to dance. This was a hell of a time to be coming up with these minor details.

As we got on the dance floor another one of those stupid minor details came up. Since I was about a foot smaller I found myself looking directly at her breasts. Somehow this didn't seem right, so I turned my head and looked at something else. The next thing I knew my head was resting on one of them, and my nose was down in the valley of those mountains. She pulled away, gave me a dirty look, and walked back to the booth to sit down. By the time I got back, she was sitting there trying to get the blood from my lip off of her blouse. When the hell is my lip going to stop bleeding?

When Judy and Ed got back from dancing, Carol came up with the fastest excuse to leave that I ever heard. "Sorry about that, Ed," I said.

"Kuni, I can't take you anywhere. You are singularly screwing up my whole summer social life here."

"Ed, you know the reason you take me with you is because I am a chick magnet, and I get all the girls for you."

"Kuni, you can screw up a wet dream."

"I don't understand. I've seen Bogart do that with the cigarette lots of times, and he never had that kind of trouble."

"Kuni, Bogart wasn't a screw up like you."

On the way home I told Ed I was sorry for messing up his chance with Judy. "No big deal," Ed said, "I wasn't that wild about her. In fact I am more interested in a girl back home. She is a girl who is the daughter of some friends of my parents. She is a year younger and I think she likes me some."

"I didn't know about that one. What is she like?"

"She is shy and real sweet. She goes to our church, so I see her every week. Kuni, there is something different about her. I don't feel the same way around her like I do around other girls."

"Ed, it sounds like there is something different with you, not her. It sounds like she is the right one for you. Don't let her get away."

"I don't know. I can talk to girls ok, but with her I freeze up and cannot find the right words. I am so afraid that she wouldn't like me and will tell me to get lost. I hope she and I can get together, Kuni, I really don't want a bunch of girl-friends, I just want one that I really care about, and I care about her."

"Ed, with my track record, I should be the last person to give advice to anyone. But I bet she is thinking the same thing that you just said. You have to let her know or else you will wonder for the rest of your life. Look at it this way, you have a 50 percent chance of getting it right. If you don't tell her you have a 100 percent chance of getting it wrong. Ed, don't be a wuss, tell her how you feel. Oh, yeah, and don't screw it up."

"Kuni, you're pretty smart for a virgin."

"Yes, I am."

CHAPTER TEN

After work, it was one of those nights when we couldn't decide what to do. Those are the nights when we usually get into trouble. We finally decided to have Paul go up to New York and get some beer. We pooled our money and found out we were dirt poor. It was only enough to get a couple of quarts of beer, but we figured that would be enough for us to go fishing.

By the time Paul got back, it was getting dark. The lake was off limits to campers after dark, but no one cared whether we drowned or not, so we more or less did what we wanted. One thing they did care about was drinking, so we decided to go over on the other side of the lake to fish. We took some fishing poles out from the back of Paul's truck and walked down the road to the other side of the lake. We couldn't see the moon or stars, so it was really dark by the time we got to where we were going to fish.

"I don't think this is such a hot idea. What the hell are we going to do with the fish if we catch any? Never mind, we never catch fish anyway," I said, but as always no one ever listened to me.

We baited our hooks and threw our lines in to fish. We put some rocks on the poles and sat back to drink and tell each other lies about how much we know about girls. Clock was sharing with us his vast knowledge on sex and the American girl.

"Clock," I said, "what do you know about girls? We are the same age, and I don't know shit about girls."

"That is because I am a lot more advanced with women than you."

"That's a crock, Clock. I am a lot cooler than you with my Bogart impression. That gets them every time."

Lats, who probably knows more than Clock, Ed and I all put together, kept telling us we were sick little perverts. Paul, who is almost living with his girlfriend, kept quiet for he knew how dumb we were when it came to girls.

Lats finally had to say, "If the three of you wrote everything down that you knew about women, you wouldn't be able to finish a sentence."

Clock was going up to the canteen tomorrow night to meet Jean, and he asked me if I wanted to come along. "Naomi is going to be there, and she was asking about you."

"Don't lie to me, Clock. Was she really? I didn't think I made a good first impression with her. In fact, the second one was worse yet."

"Don't feel too bad, Kuni. The third screw up will probably make you a legend."

"Screw you, Clock."

"Are girls all you guys think about?" Paul asked.

"Do you mean there is something else?" I answered.

"By the way, Kuni," Clock said, "Thanks for putting in a good word about me, Jean said you told Naomi I was one of the good guys, whatever the hell that means."

"I like Naomi, so put in a good word for me, ok? You owe me."

"I already did. I told Jean you were bat shit crazy and belong in a nuthouse."

"Well, you could have lied a little."

"No, Kuni, I said you were weird and you come up with all kinds of dumb shit, but I think she likes you anyway. I don't know why."

"Can you guys talk about something else besides girls?" Lats asked.

"Ok, Lats," Ed said, "Let's talk about Alice. What is she like?"

"God, it looks like I'm in charge of a day care center," Paul stated.

"I know," I said, "let's open up a beer, and then talk about girls."

So we opened one of the beers and passed it around, skipping Lats. He didn't want to get in trouble.

"Lighten up Lats," I said, "You need at least one vice so you can have something to barter with when you need help from God. How can you say to God, if you help me now I will give up this vice? You don't have any vices. What would be his incentive to help you?"

"Kuni, I have a vice. I hang out with you guys. That is probably the biggest vice there is."

"Well, we sure are not rubbing off on you. Hell, even Ed and Paul picked up some vices from us. As far as vices go, Clock is in a whole different league than us."

We sat around passing the beer and smoking, while I kept pumping Clock for more information about Naomi. "Ah, this is the life," Paul said as he took another drink. "I can really lay back and relax here."

"I hope you're not too relaxed," Ed remarked.

"Why?"

"Because our poles are floating away," Ed answered.

"Oh, shit!" Paul yelled as he was up and running down to the lake with us close behind. Clock tripped on a rock and fell into the lake. Paul stopped and I ran into him, and we both fell in the lake. As Paul sat there in the lake watching his poles float away, he was fighting a losing battle to control his temper.

Clock cried out that he broke his ankle. Paul and I got up and splashed over to Clock. I grabbed Clock on one side, and Paul got him on the other side. As we were helping him out of the lake, I slipped and went down, pulling Clock and Paul down on top of me. I was thrashing around like crazy trying to get these two big heavy idiots off me. I broke the surface screaming, "What the hell? Are you bastards trying to drown me?"

Paul was looking at me like maybe that wasn't such a bad idea after all. While Paul and I were arguing about whose fault it was, Clock yelled up at us to get him the hell out of the lake.

When we finally got him on shore, he was able to stand on his ankle and limp around on it. "This is just great," Paul said laying there soaking wet, "What the hell else could go wrong?"

"It's probably going to rain, Paul," Ed answered.

"Ed, would you shut the hell up?" we all cried in unison.

Since Clock, Paul and I were sitting there soaked and wet, we decided to call it a night. Lats and Paul helped Clock, and Ed led the way, smacking everyone with branches as he went along. After walking for about a half hour, we fell in a creek, stepped in mud, tripped over logs and rocks, and climbed over the worst terrain in the woods. It then started to rain.

"Oh shit!" Paul said, "Ed, this is all your fault, you shit. This night has been a total waste. What the hell else could go wrong?"

"Paul, I think I'm lost," Ed answered.

"Oh shit!"

"Ok everyone, the first thing we have to do is stick together." Lats explained, "First we will build a fire to get warm. Then we have to take turns standing guard, a search party should be out, in the morning, the main thing is not to panic and keep calm."

"Lats, sit down and shut up." Paul said.

"The road is just over there." Clock pointed. "I thought I heard a car just a minute ago."

In about 10 minutes we came to the road and followed it home. When we got back to the shack, five tired and wet kids were ready for bed.

"Hey, Clock, do you really think she likes me?" I said when we were all settled in to sleep.

"Oh, shut up, Kuni!" they all yelled and threw their pillows at me.

The next day after supper dishes, Clock came up to me and asked if I was going up to the canteen with him.

"Clock, if Naomi is going to be there, I'll be there even if I have to crawl up there over broken beer bottles," I answered. Even though I only got to speak to her a couple of times, I couldn't take my eyes off of her whenever I saw her walking around camp. She must think I am some kind of a nut because she was always catching me looking at her. Also the fact that on the jukebox in the canteen, there is a song with a line in it that goes, "What is love? Five feet of heaven in a ponytail." And I play that about ten times a night when I am at the canteen. Since she is five feet tall and wears a ponytail, she has to think I am totally crazy.

On the way up to the canteen with Clock, I was trying to figure out if I should charm her with my wit, cool and calm attitude, and a hint of mystery like Bogart. Or should I dazzle her with my animal magnetism and devil-may-care charm like Cagney. To tell you the truth, I was a nervous wreck.

As we approached the booth and I saw Naomi sitting there, I decided to use Bogart. Now what the hell would Bogart come up with to say to a girl? We slid in the booth and my mind came up with a complete blank. Just about that time Clock kicked my leg under the table.

"I said hi, Phil," Naomi was saying to me.

"Oh, ah, hello," was my snappy comeback. "I'm sorry, I'm not used to hearing Phil, everyone calls me Kuni."

"Would you want me to call you Kuni?"

"Oh no! Everyone calls me that, I would rather you call me Phil."

After that I kind of sat back and listened to the rest of them talking. You could say I was projecting an air of mystery, but in reality I figure the less I said, the lower my odds were of sticking my foot in my mouth.

It became obvious that I had to say something after Clock and Jean went up for a coke.

"Why don't we go up and sit on the stage?" I said.

"Yes, I would like that."

When we got on the stage, I gave her my best Bogart impression and said, "Naomi, why didn't you meet at the Paris train station?. I waited till the train took off. I was heartbroken."

"Well, Rick," she answered, "I wanted to meet you with all my heart, but fate intervened. I will always remember Paris and you."

I just stared at her.

"Phil, I loved *Casablanca* too, so I'm just as crazy as you."

"You must remember this," I said, singing the first line. She sat down at the piano and started playing.

"A kiss is just a kiss" she sang the second line.

"A sigh is just a sigh," we both joined in "The fundamental things apply, as time goes by. And when two lovers woo, they still say, 'I love you, on that you can rely, no matter what the future brings. 'As time goes by'."

We both started laughing when we finished singing it.

"Wow, what a girl," I stated. "You know, of course this makes us soul mates."

"Of course," she answered.

I asked Naomi if she would take off her glasses. She must have thought that was strange, but she took them off anyway. "Hum, just what I thought."

"What?" Naomi said.

"You have two green eyes, and they are beautiful, but your glasses hide them."

"No silly, they are brown."

"Well, at least I got the number right, but they are still beautiful."

"I think you're nuts." Naomi said laughing; she got a big kick out of that.

"Is that what you think of me? Here I thought I was making some headway."

"You are. What do you think of me?" she asked.

"Well, let me see now," I stared at her very intently. "I think you are a very classy girl. I don't have any class myself, but I can see it in other people. I also think that you must be an alien of some kind, with advanced knowledge of mind control. You've been on my mind since I first saw you, and if you don't mind me telling you, it's scary, me having a soulmate that is an alien."

"Well, thank you, kind sir, but please don't tell anyone. I'm in disguise."

We both laughed at that, but pretty soon Clock and Jean came up. Jean looked at us with a stupid grin on her face because we were cracking up.

After a while Jean poked Naomi and motioned toward the door. I turned to see this gorilla in shorts and a t-shirt stomping over to us.

"That's my brother. Please don't say anything," Naomi pleaded.

"What are you doing here?" he demanded.

"Nothing, I'm just sitting here with some friends."

"These bums are just hired help. Why don't you hang around with your own kind?"

"These are my friends, and I'll hang around with whomever I want."

"You hang around with your own kind," he said, "These kids are trash, and you do what I tell you. Find a Jewish kid to hang out with, and stay away from the hired help."

This was the same Mr. America that was with the nurse. If I felt a bit of remorse about what we did, it just went away.

"You should follow your own advice. Not all blond nurses are Jewish. Some are just hired help," I said.

"Are you messing around with my sister?" he said to me while he was giving me a dirty look.

"No," I answered.

"I don't believe you, you little runt."

I looked up at him with the meanest glare I could manage and said, "I don't much care whether you believe me or not."

"You little shit! Stay away from my sister." With that, he turned and walked away.

"Boy, I'm glad he left. I was getting ready to jump up and punch him in the kneecap. How come he is so big? Are you sure he wasn't left on your parents' doorstep?" I asked Naomi.

"No, he is really my brother. He is going to play football for Penn State this fall."

"I hope he doesn't stop you from seeing me," I said to Naomi.

"Do you want to see me again?" she asked, ever so sweetly.

"Yes I do, very much so," I said.

We spent about the next hour finding out more about one another. I found out that she was the only girl in her family, with three brothers. She lived in Queens. She was sixteen, going to be a senior and she loved classical music. She was not sure where she was going to college or what she wanted to be. She said she would probably just do what her parents told her.

"Do you always do what your parents want?"

"They tell me that it is always for my own good. I sometimes rebel, but I only get in trouble then. Since I am the only girl, with my parents and brothers, there are times I feel like I can't breathe. Enough about me, what about you?"

I told her my options were limited. I would probably escape to the Army after school was over. I was way too poor in money and grades to go to college. It looked like the only thing we had in common was that we lived on the same planet.

Clock and I walked them both back to their camping area, and I very reluctantly said good night. Going back to our shack, I knew that this was the only girl I wanted to go out with. Now I knew how Bogart felt in Casablanca. I was really happy when I was with her, but deep down there somewhere inside me, I felt sad. Even though she loved him, Bogart's girl had to leave him. Bogart loved her, but let her go at the end. Could I do the same?

CHAPTER ELEVEN

While on a break between the dinner dishes and the supper dishes, we were down on the ball field hitting a ball around. That is, Clock, Ed, and I were. We only had one ball, and the field was way too small for Paul. It was a real hot afternoon, so we decided to call it quits early. Clock had some cigarettes so we went over to the shady side of Paul's truck, Sherman the Second, and grabbed a smoke, while we watched Paul and Lats wiping down Sherman.

Now, you may think that smoking is a simple act, but it is not. There are many different ways to smoke. It's not the smoking that counts; it's how you do it. You have to light the cigarette just right (I still need lessons on that one), you have to hold the cigarette just right, you have to blow the smoke out and get rid of the butt just right. The ultimate effect of all this is to look "cool."

There are many ways to light the cigarette, but the goal is to look nonchalant while doing it. Holding the cigarette is the most important of the lot. This separates the manly way from the sissy way of smoking. The cigarette is to be held between the first and second knuckle of your trigger finger and your bad finger. This is a solid rule; any other fingers could label you as a sissy. Blowing out the smoke is to be done through the middle of your mouth, not from any sides of your mouth. Also let the smoke come out slow but steady. Too fast makes you look like you are coughing, too slow makes you look like a wimp. Throwing away the butt requires you to grasp the butt between your thumb and bad finger as if you were flicking something. This way you can flick the butt in just about any direction you want. Beginners should stick to just straight away but as you get more experience you can do it over the shoulder or out to the sides. See, I bet you thought it was just inhaling and exhaling.

Paul and Clock sat on the running boards of Sherman, while Ed and I sat facing them. We probably looked the ultimate cool smoking our cigarettes; Clock even did a real smooth flick of the butt over his shoulder. Boy, cool was just oozing from us. We were talking about our favorite topic, girls. Paul got a lot of teasing from us about the girl that came up to him and asked him if he wanted to see the hot and cold tattoos on her breast.

"Clock," I asked, "Did you ever see a girl with a tattoo?"

"No, I didn't Kuni," Clock answered "But I did hear of one that had 'Thank you. Come again' tattooed between her legs." This started all of us laughing over that.

"Are any of you guys going to get a tattoo?" I asked.

Ed and Clock said they probably would. I told them since the yearbook had me most likely to end up in jail, I didn't need the police to have an identifying tattoo to know me by.

"That doesn't matter," Clock said. "All they have to do is look for a short person."

"Asshole," I answered, giving him the finger.

"What is everyone going to do when you graduate?' Lats asked.

Ed said he was going to try to be a CPA like his dad. Paul said he was probably going to get married and get a job doing construction work. He said he liked doing that. Lats has all kinds of grants, so we know he is off to college.

"I would like to go to college also," Clock said, "The army has a college assistance program, so I will probably go into the service and try to go when I get out."

"What do you want to study in college?" Lats asked.

"I want to be a high school teacher."

Boy, everyone fell over on that.

"You being a teacher," I said, "that will be like a fox teaching chickens how to lay eggs."

All I wanted to do was go into the Army and travel.

"Paul, do you know that your truck is on fire?" Ed said calmly.

We all laughed about that too. "Paul, I'm not kidding, your truck is on fire," Ed said again. That stopped us from laughing and Paul looked at Ed more closely, then turned around and looked at his truck. By this time the canvas on the back of his truck was blazing away. Paul climbed up the truck like a mad man and started ripping away at the canvas.

"I guess we better help," Ed said as the rest of us were climbing up on the truck untying the canvas. We got the canvas on the ground and put the fire out. Paul was furious at Clock and Ed. He was mad at Ed for not telling him sooner and at Clock for flipping the cigarette up there in the first place.

Paul spent the rest of the day cursing those two, but by nightfall we finally got him to calm down. After the lights were out, and we were trying to sleep, I called over to Paul, "Hey Paul, do you know that your bed is on fire?"

"Kuni, you smart ass shut up and go to sleep," Paul answered.

The next morning everything was forgotten, and we were all back to normal—at least normal for us.

After supper dishes, Clock and I went up to the canteen. I was hoping to see Naomi again, but as I looked over the crowd I couldn't see her anywhere. Jean waved at Clock and he started over to where she was sitting, and I went over to grab a coke. As I was drinking my Coke, Naomi poked me in the ribs.

"Hi," she said when I turned around, "When did you come in?"

"I just got here," I told her, "I looked for you but I didn't see you."

"I was sitting in the booth on the other side. When I saw Clock, I was hoping you would be around."

"Do you want a Coke?" I asked her.

"Sure, do you want to find a place to sit?"

"It's awfully crowded," I said looking around. "Let's get out of here and go up stairs to the gym."

"Ok. Besides, I don't want to be here when my brother comes in. I don't think he likes you."

"I got that feeling too," I replied, "But I'm not worried about him. It's that awesome sister that I am trying to impress."

I'm sure Bogart must be around somewhere cheering me on. With that thought, I grabbed a couple of Cokes, and we went upstairs to the gym.

We walked around the gym and worked our way up to the stage, which was on the other side of the gym. On the stage they had a piano, so I walked over and sat on the stool.

"I bet you didn't know that I was a great piano player did you?" I asked. "Listen to this." I stretched my fingers and got my hands in shape while she sat on the stool with me and snickered.

I played that hard classical piece called "Chopsticks." "Well what do you think of that? I can play anything on piano. Go ahead, give me any kind of request."

"Can you play some jazz?" she asked.

"No problem." I then played that hard jazz piece called "Chopsticks." When she got her laughter under control I said, "Let me have your hands, and I will show you how to play it."

I took her hands and showed her what keys to play. After going through it a couple of times with her, I asked her to play it for me. She did, and it was the best "Chopsticks" I've ever heard.

"You're hustling me. Why didn't you tell me you could play this thing?"

"Oh, I can play a little," she answered with a wide grin on her face.

"Why didn't you say something? I feel like an idiot now. At least I got to hold your hands."

"That's why I didn't say anything," she smiled.

God, this girl is really getting to me, I thought. I asked her if she could play something nice for me.

"Most of what I know is classical music," she said. "Would you like to hear something like that?"

I said I would and she started playing. It was just beautiful. I didn't know what it was, but it was beautiful. I kept watching her face while she played, and it was like she went into another world. When she finished, I stood up and clapped.

"You little hustler! 'Oh, I can play just a little bit.' Yeah, right! You've been hustling me all along."

"Well, just like you hustle pool. See, you're not the only one."

"Boy, talk about being shot down, but that was just beautiful. You're great, do you know that?"

She smiled at me and said, "Of course."

"What was the name of that piece you played?"

"That was Beethoven's First movement from *Moonlight Sonata*."

"Nuts, I should have been able to recognize that right off. I'm one of his biggest fans. I used to listen to him all the time on the country music radio station. He plays at the Grand Ole Opry all the time. I have a song that I hope will be our song. If I tell you, will you be able to play it?"

"I know what it is," she said as she started to play "As Time Goes By." We both agreed that this would be our song.

She touched me on the shoulder and said, "Where did Clock and Jean go?"

"Clock and Jean? Who are they?"

"I better be getting back to my cabin. We have to be in by bed check."

"Do you mind if I walk you back?" I asked.

"I was hoping you would."

"What time is the bed check?" I asked.

"It's not for a couple hours, but I thought we could find a place where we can talk without my brother or the rest of the campers around. My brother can be such a jerk sometimes."

"I think I know a good spot," thinking that Paul parks his truck behind the fence between the parking lot and our shack. That way no one from the camp could see us.

PHIL MUTA

We went down the path, crossed the road, and went over to Paul's truck. I cleared a spot off in the back and helped her climb up. She slid over to me, and I put my arm around her and started telling her a little about my life and comparing how much different our lives were.

They were exactly opposite; it was like two different worlds. She was telling me how everything was planned out for her by her parents. They made her plans and if she didn't obey them that made her a bad girl. They told her who her friends were, what she watched on tv, who she hung around with, and even what she ate.

"Phil, sometimes I feel so trapped, I don't even know who I am most of the time. I tried to break free a couple times but always something bad comes from it. Being with you and away from my parents, I feel so free. But enough about me. How are *your* parents?"

"No, my parents are ok. I like them. I more or less do what I want to, and I think they expect me to do the right thing, and so far that is pretty much what I do. They tell me when supper is going to be ready, and the rest is up to me. I believe what my parents don't know won't hurt them, so I don't tell them anything."

"God, I wish my parents were like them. Sometimes they make me feel so guilty. Your parents are right. I think you always do the right thing."

"Well," I answered, "I don't want to disappoint Bogart. He thinks I am just as cool as he is"

"I think you are way cooler than Bogart, because you are sitting here with me and he isn't."

Finally I built up enough courage and leaned over and kissed her. Wow, it was never this good before. However,

90

my experience was pretty slim. When we came up for air, we looked at one another and started kissing again.

"Well, I better go in now," she said, but neither one of us moved, so I kissed her again.

"I don't really want to leave," I said.

"I know, I don't either."

So I kissed her a couple more times.

"I really should go in. Bed check will be in a little while."

We got up, and I walked her up to the girl's entrance. I brought her over in the shadows and kissed her and told her good night. We tore ourselves apart, and I started walking away.

"Phil!" I heard her say, and I turned around. She came running back to me and grabbed me around the neck and kissed me. She then turned and ran into the girl's area.

I stood there for a while trying to get my heart back to beating and my legs to get back to normal. Wow, my feelings were running wild. I never felt this way about a girl before.

I don't remember how I got back to the shack, but I walked in and Clock was there already. "Boy, we were going to start a search party for you. You two really hit it off pretty good tonight. Jean and I saw you guys sitting at the piano."

"Yeah," I answered, "I really like that girl."

"She may not be a raving beauty, but she is cute," Clock said.

"Clock, she is the most beautiful girl I've ever seen."

"Then you need those glasses she wears," Ed said.

"Screw you, Ed."

"Kuni, don't listen to those guys, they wouldn't know beauty if it hit them over the head," Paul replied.

"Well, anyway," Clock said, "Watch out for her brother. They say he's a mean son of a bitch."

"Hell, I'm going to bed. I don't give a shit about him, it's her I like, not him.

We shut the lights off, and I just lay in bed thinking about Naomi and replaying in my mind of her running over and putting her arms around my neck and kissing me. Her face was the last thing I remembered before I fell asleep.

CHAPTER TWELVE

Camp Laura was getting together a camp baseball team to play other camps. They were down on the baseball field for their practice, and we went over and talked them into playing us for practice. Seeing that there were only five of us, they were big enough to let us bat first, but that was a big mistake. What they didn't know was that Clock, Paul, and I were on the high school team in school and that all of us played baseball all summer long when we were little kids.

I led off and hit one over the third baseman's head. Ed got a single in right, putting me on third. Paul drove us all in with a home run about fifty feet over the center fielder's head. Lats hit a double in left, and Clock hit a homer in the woods. I came up and hit another one in the woods, but it bounced in, so they ruled it a ground rule double. Ed drove me in with another double. Paul then came up and hit a ball completely over the trees and landed on the roof of the guest house. That ball must have gone at least 475 feet.

The Camp Laura baseball team quit. Before supper the word was spread around the camp about Paul's homer, and it was up to 600 feet by then. The coach of the team wanted Paul to play on the camp team, but since he wasn't a camper or Jewish, the rules wouldn't allow it. However, we did try to convince him to convert. Once again the camp marveled at Paul's mighty power. Paul thought the whole thing was silly.

A couple mornings later we were sitting down eating breakfast when Alice and her mom asked us if we wanted to come up to their farm Saturday night and roast some hotdogs and marshmallows. "We have a nice area by the creek where we could build a fire," Alice said. "Come on, it will be fun."

Well, with something like that, we don't need to be asked twice. "That sounds like a great idea," Paul said.

"Do you trust us not to burn down your farm?" I asked Alice's mother.

"I'll have everyone watch you carefully," she laughed.

"We can bring the kosher dogs and marshmallows," Clock said. He then leaned over to me and whispered that the camp would be glad to donate all that, plus the buns and chips. I told him I would help him sneak the stuff out.

An idea came to me and I asked Alice if we could bring our girl friends. The whole table stopped talking and just looked at me.

"What?" I said "Well, I will have one as soon as I can talk her into it."

Alice asked her mother, and she just smiled and said it was ok with her. Alice's mother always liked me best. Paul told Alice and her mom that we would come and it was very kind of them to invite us out.

"Alice," I said, "If I was sure you would turn out like your mother I would ask you to marry me. You're too nice to waste your time on Lats when you can have me instead."

"Well, I don't want to get in the way between you and your girlfriend. You know, the one that doesn't know it yet," Alice said.

"That is cruel, Alice. You broke my heart."

As we were getting ready for the campers to finish their breakfast I grabbed Clock and told him that I got the girls invited, and it was up to him to get his devious mind working and figure out a way to get them there. "Since it's Saturday night, the girls wouldn't have to be in 'til late. You should be able to come up with something sneaky by then," I said.

"Ok, I'll see if I can talk to Jean some time today and see if they will go along with it," he answered.

Clock asked Jean that afternoon, and they thought it was a great idea, so that night we were huddled on the stage of the canteen planning our trip for tomorrow.

It was decided that the girls would go up to the canteen and then skip out early, and by that time we should have been through with the supper dishes and showers. They would sneak down to the linen storage building and wait for us. That building was right on a curve and out of site from the main camp. Once we rounded that curve, the girls would come over to the truck and jump in the back. Getting back would be the same way. They would leave the back window open in their bunks and climb in that way. I sometimes wonder if it is illegal to be as smart as we are. I bet Bogart or Cagney would have been proud of me. If Bogart had me around, Ingrid Bergman would have met him at the train station.

Saturday came and, finally, suppertime. Now if only the little brats would hurry up and eat. Since this was the weekend, we also had to wait until the guests finished eating. The guests were mostly the parents of the campers or guests of the owners. They usually ate last and then sat around smoking and talking, but still we had to sit there and wait until they finished. Paul finally got tired of our bellyaching and said to hell with it, so we decided to leave the dishes stacked and do them in the morning.

We took off and ran down to take quick showers and get ready. In about a half hour, we were piling into the truck, with Clock and I in the back to get the girls. As we rounded the curve out of sight of the camp, the girls ran over and jumped in the back.

"Did you have any trouble getting away?" I asked.

"No, but we didn't think you were coming," Naomi answered.

"I know. We got hung up waiting for the parents to finish eating. Besides, you know it would take an extreme act of nature to keep me away from you."

Clock and I had gotten most of the stuff from the kitchen this afternoon. We didn't ask anyone because we knew they would want us to have it anyway. As always, who could resist a sweet bunch of guys like us? Lats and Alice had gone on ahead of us in Alice's car to buy what we couldn't steal—I mean, what we were going to sample to make sure it was good enough for the campers.

When we turned off the main road, we drove about a mile and a half up the gravel road and pulled into a pasture. We bounced and jarred our way to the creek where Lats and Alice were. I wanted Paul to go back and ride in again. I was enjoying having Naomi bouncing around with me holding her.

The spot couldn't have been better. The creek had what looked like a small beach; it was a cleared sandy spot that came back from the water about twenty feet. It looked like an opening about twenty by thirty feet with trees around it. The sand was more like really small pebbles, and there was a fire pit in the middle of the clearing. We carried over some logs from the woods for the girls to sit on. It was everyone's job to gather up some wood for burning. Naomi and I went down the stream a little way and came up to a fence with cows in the pasture on the other side of the fence. At this time of the night, they were probably finished with the milking and put out in the pasture for the night. There was no bull around, and it didn't look like there were any young cows in the group, so I tried to talk Naomi into climbing over the fence. Well, she didn't think too much of that idea at all. I climbed over on the other side and asked her to come over to the fence.

"See, there is nothing to be afraid of," I said. And after some talking to her, she finally got up enough nerve to walk over to the fence. When she got to the fence, a cow decided to come over and see what was going on. The next thing I knew she was back from the fence by about fifty feet.

"Oh come on, look," I said as I walked over to the cow. I talked to the cow a little and she let me get close enough to pet her on the head. "See, they are just cows. They wouldn't hurt you."

"Are they bulls?"

"No, these are just milking cows, and they are real gentle."

"Ok, but you have to protect me and let them bite you first," she said, and she slowly came back to the fence. I went over and helped her climb over.

I kept hold of her hand, and we walked over to the cow. I took her hand and patted the cow's head. She giggled about that, and the next thing I knew, she had both hands on the cow, and she was having a ball petting her cow. While the two of them were getting to know one another, I went and got some wood. Prying her away from the cow, we went back to the group.

"I petted a cow," was the first thing Naomi said when she saw Jean. The next thing we knew, all the girls went back so Jean could pet one also.

While they were doing that we set up the fireplace and got a good fire going. There was enough wood that we gathered to last us the rest of the night. Lats and Ed cut up some sticks to roast the hot dogs and marshmallows.

By the time Alice got back with the girls, we had everything set up. Clock, Lats, and I roasted some hot dogs for the girls and ourselves, and we sat around eating and talking and in general having a great time. It was dark by the time we had gotten to the marshmallows, and we were stuffed and relaxed after those.

Paul got up and put some more logs on the fire. I lay back against a log with Naomi lying up against me with her head on my chest, and we were both watching the fire. Let's face it, I was in heaven. I was sure that heaven was just like this.

We were sitting around talking about our vast wealth of experience, at least what we could gather in sixteen years of childhood, when the subject got around to Nick's. Nick's is a newsstand, to everyone's amazement, owned by a man named Nick. We all kind of look after Nick because he is blind. We help him out when he needs help, and we make sure that no one steals from him. In return he lets us hang out in his place where we sit around and tell lies and smoke and just be obnoxious as we can.

"Kuni, why don't you tell us one of those weird stories of yours?" Clock said.

"Phil," Naomi said, "A weird story coming from you? Why am I not surprised?"

"Naomi, you may not believe this," Clock said, "but Kuni is famous with the little kids and some of the parents in the neighborhood. Friday night back home the kids would sit around the light under the streetlight and want Kuni to tell them a story. Some of the parents would bring chairs and listen to them also."

"Is this true?" Naomi asked.

"Well," I answered, "I like to read books a lot, so I just tell some of the stories from them. They like to hear scary ones the best, and then the parents get mad at me when it's the kids' bedtime."

"It's funny," Clock added, "the kids are sitting under the streetlight and as Kuni tells the story they keep moving to the middle of the light. Sometimes the boys would try to push the girl outside of the light."

"Now I know why Naomi likes you." Jean said.

"More and more," Naomi smiled as she looked at me. "Now you have to tell us one."

"Ok, gather around little children and I will tell you the story of old Jake the farmer and the traveling salesman," I said as everyone shut up and started to listen.

"Well, old Jake had a small farm not too far from here. Now, Jake was a bitter, evil old man who never had much of anything. He usually blamed this on everyone else, but the fact that he was lazy and drank too much was the reason for it. Jake always thought that he should be rich and could not understand why everyone else always had more than him. But one dark, stormy night not too long ago changed everything for Jake.

"It had rained for about three days off and on, and that day it rained the hardest. Just up the road from Jake's place, a mudslide had taken out a large section of the road. The rain had slacked off to just a drizzle when old Jake heard a knock on the door."

Just about that time everyone moved a little closer to the fire, as the night noises seemed to disappear and only the sounds from the fire could be heard. "A man appeared at the door," I went on, "claiming that he was a salesman and was blocked off from town by the mudslide. He said he would be willing to pay for a night's lodging if Jake would put him up. Well, old Jake, never being one to turn down money, put him up in his room. The man was holding on to his sample case and would not let go of it when Jake offered to carry it upstairs for him.

"Now, Jake was a curious old man but could not draw out of the man what was in the sample case. After Jake set him up in the room and left, he quietly came back and peeked in the keyhole. Before the man got ready for bed, he opened the sample case to check out the contents inside. Well, old Jake nearly fainted because the inside of that case was loaded with industrial diamonds.

"Jake sat up for hours after that and thought of how he had to have those diamonds. He finally decided that he would murder the man and bury his body. When they found his car, they would figure he abandoned it and got lost in the storm. Jake didn't have a gun and thought of a knife, but he was afraid if he didn't kill him the first time, the man would be able to take the knife away from him. Then an idea came to him, his ax, which would surely kill the man on the first blow for he kept it sharp.

"Now, where did he leave that ax? Oh yes, he remembered he used it to chop wood last. He must have left it in the wood shed. Old Jake put on his raincoat and went out in the mud and rain to get it. All the while, he was thinking of all those diamonds and how he could spend all the money from them.

"He was still thinking of that as he slowly climbed the stairs holding on to the ax," I tried to make my voice as scary as I could. Let's face it. I was really getting into having Naomi hanging on to me.

"Slowly," I continued, "Jake climbed up the dark stairs and stood before the bedroom door. It creaked as he opened it, and he slipped into the room. Without moonlight, the room was especially dark. Jake stood over the sleeping form on the bed and raised the ax over his head. The salesman must have sensed something was wrong because he opened his eyes at that time. Seeing the ax coming down upon him, he yelled and brought up his hand by instinct to warn off the blow. He felt a sharp, quick pain as the ax severed his hand. He screamed and screamed, not even realizing the second blow as it struck his head. With a flashing bright light, his scream faded away, and he died."

Naomi shuddered and hugged me tighter. "I don't want to hear any more," she said.

"Oh, that was the worst part, the rest is ok now," I answered.

The rest of them wanted me to continue, so Naomi said ok as long as there wasn't any more gory stuff. I got up to throw some more wood on the fire, and Naomi got up with me and hung on. I can't say I wasn't enjoying every second of this. We moved the logs closer to the fire, mostly for the warmth because the night was getting colder. As we all settled back down again, I went on.

"Old Jake was shaking after that. He didn't know it was going to be that bad. The screaming, he could still hear it as he stood there staring at the hand by his foot. I have to bury it, he thought as he tried to get his brain working again. He cleaned up as much as he could around the body and placed the hand with the body. He wrapped the sheet around the body and started dragging the body down stairs and outside.

"He took the body around the back where he started to dig a grave. It was hard work because of the ground being so wet, but he kept digging while still hearing the sounds of screaming in his head. When he got the hole deep enough, he placed the body down in it. Something is wrong, he thought. The hand—it wasn't there.

"He retraced his steps and found the hand about forty feet away. He picked up the hand, but didn't notice the strange trail the hand made crawling back to the house. When he got back to the grave, he tried to drop the hand in, but it wouldn't let go of his own hand. 'That can't be!' he cried as he began pulling it off with his other hand. Finally, it came loose and dropped in the grave. Jake was near panic. He was shaking so hard as he covered the grave as fast as he could. Running back to the house, he kept feeling that hand on him. He sank into a chair dripping wet and trembling. After a while he started feeling better and went up to the bedroom. Taking out the sample case he spread the diamonds on the bed. They're all mine he thought, all mine, I'm rich. Putting them back, he suddenly realized how tired he was. Sleep, that's what he needed. Putting another sheet on the bed, he laid down and fell asleep almost immediately.

"Waking up with a start, he tried to get out of bed, but he couldn't move. His arms and feet felt so heavy that he couldn't lift them. The room was so dark and quiet, he thought, but he heard something. A voice, that's what it was. A voice woke him up. Not just a voice, more like a cry. Again he heard it, the sound coming from outside. It was a cry, no, a plea. He tried to get up again, but still he could not move. Then he heard another noise, this one in the house. Something was crawling up the stairs. He could hear the noise outside louder now. 'My hand,' it cried. It seemed to be under his window now. 'My hand, where is my hand'? It kept saying over and over again.

"Jake again tried to get up, but still he could not move. That other noise, it was in his room now. It was trying to climb up the foot of his bed. Then he saw that black dirty hand come over the foot of his bed, crawling closer and closer to him. Meanwhile the voice outside the window was still crying out, 'My hand, where is my hand?'

"Here it is," I hollered as I grabbed Naomi's neck with my hand. That girl must have screamed loud enough for the whole state to hear, as she jumped about three feet straight up. Then I realized that the other girls were screaming too. Naomi started beating on me, and we rolled around on the sand with me laughing. None of the girls wanted to hear any more stories, so we just talked and roasted more marshmallows.

Alice got Lats to try to bring us back tomorrow afternoon, and she would show us around the farm. The girls had canoeing lessons and couldn't make it.

We put the fire out and walked back to the truck. When we climbed up in the truck, I took Naomi up front and on the way back we held on to each other, not wanting the night to end. At least I didn't.

Paul stopped the truck at the same spot where we were to drop the girls off, but they said no way, and we had to walk them back to their bunks. At least to the back of them. When we got them there, we kissed them goodnight and they crawled through the window. Naomi stuck her head back out the window and told me she had a great time and that she would probably have nightmares now thanks to me. She touched the side of my face, kissed me, and then backed in, closing the window.

"Clock, I'm in love," I said as we walked back to our shack.

"No, Kuni, everyone knows that you're just plain crazy."

"Yes, I am."

CHAPTER THIRTEEN

On Sunday morning during the breakfast dishes, our boss Ruth came over and told Paul that she wanted to see him in the office after dishes. Well, we thought we had it. For sure, someone found out about us taking the girls with us last night. We sat around waiting for Paul to get back to see how much trouble we were in. Paul came back madder than a bull. He threw down his apron and yelled, "Bullshit!" Now that language was about the strongest we ever heard from him, so we knew he was really pissed.

"Did they find out about the girls?" Clock asked.

"No it's not that. She was mad about the dirty dishes we left last night. Some of the busboys didn't like the idea of waiting around for the guests to finish while we left," Paul answered.

"Oh hell, is that all?" I said, quite relieved. "What the hell do we care what the busboys don't like?"

"That isn't all," Paul added. "She told the busboys that they didn't have to wait until all the guests were finished. She said that we will have to wait until they finish, and we will have to clear off the tables until everyone leaves."

"That's not fair!" we all answered together.

"Ok," Paul said, "Let's wait and see how tonight goes, and then we will hold a council of war."

By that afternoon we had forgotten all about our little set down, and we were anxious about going up to Alice's farm. This time we were going up to see the house instead of just a pasture.

We had to drive through the populated area of the city of Deep Forge to get to their farm. We must have just missed the rush hour because we didn't see a soul. Since we had to drive on this long gravel road to get to their house, it was noted that Sherman II not only was missing a muffler but it seemed that springs were another option that Sherman II came without. No one said anything about it because we didn't want to hurt Sherman II's feelings.

Their farmhouse was a big old white home that looked kind of comfortable. The yard had quite a few trees in it and the house sat back some from the road. The front had a big porch that covered the whole front. It had a big porch swing on it, some steps, and a couple of chairs. Alice's mom and dad were sitting in the chairs, Alice was sitting on the steps, and a stupid cat had the whole swing to herself. There was another porch on the side of the house. This porch was facing the driveway and looked like that was the porch that gets all the use. Their barn was set back from the house about two hundred feet with the driveway continuing down to it. It was a large barn that looked like it held about seventy head of dairy cows. I know because I was raised on a dairy farm until I was about nine years old. I also spent many summers and weekends helping out with the milking and haying on my grandmother's dairy farm. So as soon as I got to know Alice and her mother, their farm was the center of my conversation with them.

Looking around the farm, I could see the love and care they put into the place. After a while, any farm takes on the characteristics of the people who take care of it. We knew Alice and her parents were quality people, but even if I didn't, their farm would have told me so. The whole area looked like something Grandma Moses would have painted.

We stood for a while on the front porch and talked to Alice's parents. After we had some iced tea and got to know Alice's father, who was a little quiet but seemed nice, Alice showed us around the farm.

Paul got chased out of the chicken coop by a chicken trying to peck him, so we didn't spend too much time there. "Paul," I said, "females just can't leave you alone."

"Shut up, Kuni," he answered.

Alice showed us the barn and silo and some other outbuildings that stored their equipment. She also showed us two of their workhorses, and they were big Morgan horses. Alice pointed to one she called Beau and said that she rides that one around the farm all the time. Right away Ed wanted to ride that one, and he kept pestering Alice to let him ride. Well, after he assured Alice that he could ride a horse as good as a horse fly, Alice let him ride Beau.

With Alice holding on to the horse, Paul threw Ed up on the horse's back. With the added weight on his back, the horse started walking away, and true to form, Ed rode him like a horse fly. His arms were wrapped around the horse's neck and he hung on for his life. It didn't take the horse long to realize that he was smarter than the idiot on his back, so he just went where he wanted to.

While Ed and his horse were horsing around, pardon the pun, we went up to the side porch and sat down. I guess the horse thought he was invited because he decided to join us. We all sat around watching Ed hang on to the horse yelling, "Whoa, whoa!" We all thought that the horse was going to stop at the porch, but when the horse started climbing the stairs, we all decided to let him have the porch. As we scattered in different directions, Alice was grabbing the mare of the horse trying to get the horse off the porch. The horse, figuring he got this far, was trying to get in the house, and poor Ed was just trying to hang on yelling, "Whoa boy, whoa boy!"

Finally Alice got the horse off the porch, and by now, the horse knew he was in some kind of trouble. So he took off for the safety of the barn with Ed's arms still wrapped around his neck yelling, "Whoa boy, whoa boy!" Before the horse got to the barn, Ed decided to jump off. Well, the way his luck was going, he landed in some cow shit. After that we wouldn't let him back on the porch.

Milking time came, and we all went to the barn. Paul and I were about the only ones that had been around a farm, so the rest of the gang wasn't too familiar with the cows. Alice's father let us have a cow apiece to milk by hand. Now I've been on farms a lot, but, mind you, I am not the greatest milker going. At least I knew how to squeeze a teat, which is more than I can say for the rest.

This was Ed's first time in a barn. Everyone realized that at once when we walked into the barn, and Ed stepped in a cow turd and then asked what that little ditch in the back of the cows was for.

Paul, Alice and I proceeded to give the rest of them lessons in milking. God, I don't understand how they could miss that pail so much. Ed was doing ok after a while until the cow next to Ed lifted his tail and peed. Ed jumped off the stool and started screaming that the cow tried to pee on him.

Clock took to milking pretty fast. If it has to do with a female, Clock learns fast. Alice was working with Lats on a cow, and like anything else he picked it up with no trouble. Alice did have to tell me to quit squirting the cats.

After we had mastered the technique of milking a cow, we decided to get out of there before Ed started to milk a bull. It was getting late, and we still had to get back for supper dishes. Besides that, at the rate Ed was falling or stepping in shit, we figured we better leave before he drowned in it. We made him keep his distance on the way back and told him to leave his clothes outside.

Of course we couldn't let him off that easily. We kept harassing him about being able to ride like a horse fly. "Ed," I said, "You were right about being a fly. I could tell because you were always around cow shit."

After supper dishes, I went up to the canteen hoping to see Naomi. She was sitting with Jean and came over when she saw me. She wanted to go sit in the back of Paul's truck, so we walked down the path to the fence and climbed up in the back of the truck..

"Well, Phil, did you guys have a good time at the farm today?"

"Yeah, Ed was showing us how to ride a horse. He even showed us how to get a horse to climb up porch steps."

I told her about all the things we did that afternoon and all of Ed's troubles.

"You guys are weird," she said. "You are so crazy. I wish I was with you today."

"Yeah, I'm the only sane one there."

"That is highly debatable. I would say Lats is the only sane one."

"Well, he does hang around me a lot so I must be a good example for him. Ok, why do people roll their eyes when I say something? See you just did it again."

We held hands and kissed a few times.

"Phil, I want to know a little more about you. Did you really tell stories to the kids or was Clock just joking with us?"

"You didn't like the story I told the other night?"

"No, and I still haven't forgiven you for that. I was afraid to fall asleep that night."

"If you would have said something, I would have come over and tucked you in and stayed there to protect you."

"I don't doubt that all. Do you really read stories to the kids?"

"Yes, I like to read a lot and the kids like to hear some of the stories. I think some of them are starting to read also."

"Phil, that is awesome. Every day I find more reasons to like you."

"Naomi, I have my own selfish motives. You may not like me when you hear the other reason I tell those stories."

"And what is that?"

"A couple houses up from my house, there is a girl about 30 who is divorced with a little girl, and they live with her mother. She sometimes comes out with her little girl and listens to the stories. I think every one of us boys past puberty has a mad crush on her."

"Why does everyone have a crush on an older woman?"

"First of all she is nice, we all think she is beautiful, and she dresses sexy as hell, but it's not exactly a crush, it's more like a quest."

"What?"

"Now, don't tell anyone but boys are idiots really, and I'm probably the worst. The rumor going around is that Susie, that is her name, has a birthmark shaped like a heart on one of her butt cheeks. It is the quest of every boy there to see that. I am sure I would only see that in my dreams, but so far it hasn't happened. So far I don't think anyone has seen it yet. But all boys need a goal."

"So Phil, are you telling me you are a pervert?"

"Yes, but a nice well meaning one. What happened to that awesome thing?

"It is still there, but it has some rough edges to it. All boys are perverts, but you are not a boy, you are a nice man."

"Naomi, I gave up that quest as soon as I saw you. I have a new one now."

"Phil, you are not going to see my butt."

CHAPTER FOURTEEN

That night we waited until 9 o'clock when the guests finally left. Boy, we were hot. While I gathered up the dishes, I said to myself, "Of course they know this means war." I reminded everyone that we were going to have a council of war after work tonight. It was time to come up with a battle plan.

The guests are usually parents of some of the campers, and it was becoming apparent to us that these people were our enemies. The reason was simple enough; when the campers ate, they would sit down, eat, and then leave. But the guests were different. They would take their time eating and then sit around smoking, drinking, and talking. Meanwhile we had to stand around in the kitchen and wait until they left and then go in to pick up the dishes and wash them.

When we got back to our shack, I told them I could not believe that with our devious minds we could not come up with some diabolical plan to rid ourselves of this trouble. We began to get our brains in gear to come up with some ideas. After throwing out some of the obvious but extreme ideas of killing them all off, we finally settled on a few simple things with the salt and pepper shakers and the sugar containers. We figured we would try those next weekend and see if that would do us any good.

The next night we all went up to the canteen. It had been over 24 hours since I had seen Naomi, and I was starting to go into withdrawals. When we walked into the canteen, Naomi saw me and came over.

"Hi," she said. "I was beginning to think I wouldn't see you again."

"Clock and I were planning to come up here last night but we had to work 'til after nine." I answered.

"We thought you guys were avoiding us."

"Are you kidding?" I whispered to her. "I'm becoming addicted to you. My attention span is down to three minutes, and then I start thinking about you."

"Good, I like to be on your mind."

Clock and Jean were at the counter talking while Paul and Ed were playing a pinball machine. So we decided to go down to Sherman II and sit in the back of the truck.

"You don't mind sitting in the back of Sherman II, do you?"

"Are you kidding, I love this truck," she answered. "It's becoming my favorite spot in the camp. Last Tuesday I came down here and took some pictures of Sherman II."

"You're kidding."

"I know, you think I'm crazy."

"No, I just wish you liked me as much as you like Sherman II."

"I like Sherman II because of you."

I sat there with Naomi and was telling her about our brush with the guests. Telling her about some of the stupid things we come up with made her smile.

"Hey, don't laugh, we are the experts when it comes to doing stupid things. We set the bar so high that no one can come close," I said.

"You guys are nuts! Do you always do crazy things like that?"

"Yes, we do."

"How long have you guys known one another?" Naomi asked.

"Hey, what is this? You don't want to hear about us. We really are kind of boring."

"Not at all," she answered. "In fact all the girls think you guys are hot stuff."

"Oh, come on now. We need names and sworn statements."

"Ha! Don't get your hopes up too high. I told them all to keep their hands off you," she said sweetly.

"Now I know you are feeding me a line," I said, trying to look disappointed.

"Come on, you still didn't answer my question. How long have you known one another?"

"Well," I thought, "I really don't know. It seems like we have always known each other. Usually there are always a couple of us together when we get in trouble. That rarely happens though because we are such a nice well-behaved group."

"Now who is feeding whom the line?" she laughed. "Tell me some of the things you did that got you in trouble."

"Well there was that one time when Ron, Clock, Ed, and I put a bomb in the movie theater."

"What? No, you didn't do that," she said, looking at me. "Did you?"

"Yes, we did as a matter of fact. Only it wasn't a bomb that went 'boom'. It was a bomb that stunk."

"Tell me about it," she said as she leaned across the table towards me.

"Well, I guess the place to start is with Nick's," I began. "Nick's NewsStand is a little shack that is our hangout back home. Nick's, you might say, is on the wrong side of the tracks or town or whatever. It's all of that. Our town has a railroad cutting it almost in half. The railroad tracks follow the river; actually it is just a creek. Anyway, joining these two parts of town is a bridge running up over the railroad tracks and creek. On our side of the bridge, we had the older and poorer section of town. We also have Nick's right at the end of the bridge. We kind of felt it was an outpost, sort of guarding our side of town.

"Now, you may find this hard to believe, but as I said before, Nick's by a strange coincidence was owned by a blind man named Nick, which accounted for the fact that we were allowed to hang out there. If he knew what a sorry looking bunch of bums we were, he would have thrown us out long ago. No, I'm just kidding…Nick really was a nice guy and we made sure no one took advantage of him.

"On the other side of the bridge is what they call the classy side of town. And just at the end of the bridge there is a hang out called the Red Top, and that is where the classy kids hang out. Those of us who hang out at Nick's are considered the troublemakers, wise guys, bullies, and the ones who when we grow up will be criminals, bums, and good for nothing. Now the kids that hang around at the Red Top are the cream of the crop. They are the honor students, the big sports jocks, the well-to-do, and the general all-around good guys.

"This doesn't bother us at all except the Red Top has one thing that we don't have: girls. If you talk about injustice in this world, that has to be the worst case of injustice there is.

But for reasons completely unknown to us, there isn't a girl in town that would be caught dead in Nick's. Now, are you beginning to get the picture?"

"Yes," she said, "I think I can see why girls don't hang around there, and I bet you blame the Red Top."

"Exactly," I explained. "If it wasn't for the Red Top, we would have girls falling all over us."

She had a real good laugh about that. I don't think she believed me.

"Well," I went on, "needless to say we didn't care too much for the Red Top. We would go over to the next town and tell the tough kids that we are from the Red Top, and we would beat the hell out of them if they ever came in there. Naturally, they go there every chance they get. I bet the kids from the Red Top can't understand why everyone comes in there from out of town looking for a fight. That's our little private joke on them.

"To continue with my story, this friend of ours named Ronnie came up with a bottle of ammonia sulfate or something like that. He got it from chemistry class. I wouldn't say he stole it. He just found it in his hands when class was over. That stuff is bad, it smells like rotten eggs and it is potent. Ronnie had about a pint of the stuff, so Ronnie, Clock, Ed, and I kept it till the right time came around. Well, the right time came one Sunday night when a good movie was playing in the town next to ours. We found out that some of the kids from the Red Top were taking dates to it.

"Now, it was up to us to go and make sure that these sweet, innocent girls were safe from the evil clutches of their dates. Ronnie hid the bottle in his jacket, and the four of us went to the movies. We sat downstairs in the back seats.

About an hour into the movie we passed the bottle over to Ed who was sitting in the aisle seat. He placed the bottle on the floor, took the lid off and tipped it over. With his finger he gently started the bottle rolling down the aisle with the liquid dripping out. We had to get up and leave, the smell was so bad. I don't know how many dirty looks we got. We went into the back by the lobby and watched. Pretty soon everyone from the front moved to the back, then they moved to the balcony, after that they moved outside. It took about a half hour to clear everyone out of the movie. We left with everyone else. Before we went, Clock and I went up to the window and asked for our money back. We told them the movie stunk. And believe it or not, they gave us our money back. While we were waiting, I mentioned to Clock that I bet the gang from the Red Top had something to do with that. Clock agreed and said as soon as he saw all those guys come in he knew they were up to something. The cashier was listening to every word.

"We got back to Nick's and we all went up to the middle of the bridge and waited. Pretty soon our town police cars and two from Carbondale pulled up to the Red Top and went storming in. They put everybody in the place in those police cars and took them to the station house in Carbondale.

"I know that was a mean, vicious, rotten, miserable, under-handed thing to do but it was so much fun."

"That is terrible! How could you guys do something that mean?"

"Well, Naomi, as Dickens would say, it was the best of times, it was the worst of times—best for us, worst for them. The times called for desperate measures, but we never thought it would stink so bad. It was sweet getting our revenge with the Red Top, but we all felt guilty about the other people in the movie."

"Well, what happened to them?" she asked.

"They took them to the station house and questioned them almost all night. Their parents had to come down and get most of them. It didn't take the police too long to get to us. Of course the kids from the Red Top guessed right away that we must have done it. We do everything else."

"That Monday they came to the school and took us four away. They spent the rest of the day questioning us; each one of us in a separate room but no one broke. To this day they still don't know who did it, so don't tell them."

"You know, of course, that you guys are rotten," Naomi said.

"Yes, but revenge feels so good. I like to think Bogart would have been proud of me. How about you? What crazy things do you do?"

"Well, I don't normally do crazy things. I wish I had a place like Nick's to hang out in," she half smiled. "I would be reprimanded for just saying 'hang out.'"

"What do you do after school? Don't you get together with your girlfriends?"

"Oh, yes. We have fun," Naomi continued. "But I really don't have much time for all that. Not with piano lessons, homework and stuff. My parents wouldn't let me go out except occasionally. I'm the only girl in the family, and I guess I get somewhat overprotected. When I did get to go out I tried to squeeze in as much fun as I could. I was naïve enough to think that boys meant what they said. The only thing I was ever good for was to hurt everyone."

"How did you hurt everyone?" I asked, but she didn't hear me. Her mind was somewhere else, and the sadness was back in her face.

"I didn't mean to hurt my parents," she went on. "They love me and they said that they only wanted what was best for me. I wasn't killing anything. It was time to let the past go. But I felt so hurt and lost."

What the hell is going on here? I thought. *Those are tears there.*

"Hey," I said as I put my arms around her and hugged her. We stayed like that for about 5 minutes, and she calmed down. "I lost you. Come on back, okay?"

"Oh, I'm sorry," she said somewhat surprised, "I guess I got carried away. You must think I'm terrible."

"No, I don't," I said, still holding on to her hands, "Right now I think you are the nicest girl I have ever known. These are all new feelings for me. I want to hold you and hug you and protect you and make you smile and laugh. I want to make you feel like you made me feel. Boy, that sounded dumb. I'm sorry, disregard these ramblings of an idiot."

"Oh Phil, you are not an idiot, you are the nicest, sweetest boy I know. Right now, I think you are the thing that I need the most in my life."

"Well, I am here if you want me. Just whistle. You know how to whistle, doll, just put your lips together and blow."

She wrapped her arms around my neck, "Oh Phil, you and Bogart, two cool guys for the price of one. Right now I need you both more than anything."

Boy, I wish I understood what this girl was talking about. But I didn't figure this was the time for her to explain anything to me, so I just held on to her.

For what seemed like a long while we just sat there not saying much. I know I should have done something to make her smile, but I knew if I opened my mouth somehow my foot would find its way there.

"Phil, I wish I had met you a year ago," she finally said, and then she smiled and said, "Hey, let's go back up to the canteen and I'll play you a game on the pinball machine."

"Ok, but you better be prepared to be massacred because they don't call me the pinball wiz for nothing."

We got up to the canteen and played. I got massacred. She not only beat me but it was a humiliating loss.

"Ouch. Well, I'm just not going to pay them anymore to call me a pinball wiz," I replied. "Ok, I guess that the loser has to buy Cokes."

We went over to the counter and I got a couple cokes. We were sitting there talking when Naomi's brother came in.

He walked over to her and said, "I thought I told you to stay away from these bums."

"And I told you to leave me alone," Naomi answered, keeping her voice as low as she could.

"Why? So you can get in trouble again? The least you can do is be with your own kind of people," he replied. This guy was definitely getting on my nerves.

"Ritchie, please," she said. "These are my friends, and I like them."

Ritchie. So that's his name. Well, I could tell it would be a waste of time to make friends with this guy.

"You," he turned to me, "I thought I told you to stay away from my sister!"

"Well, I don't want to," I answered. "And I'm not going to let some asshole like you tell me what to do."

"Why you little punk!" he yelled and reached over, grabbed me, and threw me up against the wall so fast I didn't have time to react.

He took me by the shirt and stuck his face up to mine and was saying something to me. The only thing I remember was that his breath smelled like liquor. "Boy," I thought, "this guy is drunk and if he hits me, I've had it."

The next thing I knew Paul and Clock were standing on each side of him.

"Before you do anything else, you better back off, or we'll move you off," Paul said to him.

He let go of me and turned to Paul and Clock. "Is it going to take the both of you?"

"I don't think Paul needs any help with you, but if he does I'll be there," Clock answered.

"So you guys think you're tough, huh?" Ritchie said.

Paul stepped up and got into his face and said, "You lay your hands on him again, and you'll find out how tough we are."

He finally got a good look at Paul and stepped away. "Get back to your cabin," he turned and said to Naomi.

Before I could say anything, she came over to me, and I could see her eyes were filled with tears. She was trying so hard not to cry, and it was at that moment I knew that I loved her.

"I better go Phil, I'm sorry," she said.

They walked out and everything started getting back to normal. I walked over to Clock and Paul, and said, "Thanks, guys."

"You better watch out for him," Paul said. "He hates you for some reason. Can't you stay away from his sister?"

"No, Paul," I answered, "Never, I don't care how much he hates me."

"Then be careful, you little idiot," Paul replied. "I don't want you getting hurt."

It would be worth it, I thought, this feeling I have for her would be worth anything. I kept seeing her trying to hold back the tears, and I wanted to tell her how I felt.

But most of all, I wanted to climb up on a chair and smack her brother in the mouth.

Back in the shack Clock and Paul came over to my bed and talked to me.

"Kuni, I know you like this girl," Clock said, "but Jean told me that Richie dominates Naomi, and he is a mean sonofa-bitch. Knowing this, do you still want to see her?"

"Clock, I am falling in love with her."

"You poor sap, you never do anything the easy way, do you," Paul said, "Well Clock and I will make sure you are going to be ok. You go see her all you want, because I think she feels the same about you. I don't say this very often, but if he bothers you again, he will answer to me."

"Besides," Clock added, "we are not going to let anything happen to our little buddy."

CHAPTER FIFTEEN

The next night I went back up to the canteen to see Naomi, but she didn't come in all night. In fact, she didn't show up for the rest of the week. I was going to ask Jean what was going on, but she kept meeting with Clock at other places. I was beginning to realize that not only was Naomi avoiding me, but Jean was also. Saturday afternoon I finally saw Jean with some of her friends at the canteen.

She saw me come in, and she came over to me and said. "Phil, let's go up to the gym and talk."

When we got upstairs, I finally said "Okay, Jean, what's up? Where is Naomi, and why are you and her avoiding me?"

"I'm sorry, Phil."

"That was the last thing Naomi said to me and now you are saying the same thing. Is this a new disease or what? Just what is it you and Naomi are sorry about?"

Jean looked like she wished she were somewhere else. I think I knew then what she didn't want to tell me.

"Naomi doesn't want to see you again." Jean said. "I'm so sorry, Phil. I didn't want to have to tell you that."

Damn, I wish she wouldn't have told me that, I thought. I sat down on the stool trying to say something but I couldn't think of a thing.

"You're serious?" I finally said.

"Naomi didn't want to tell you. She was afraid she couldn't do it."

"Why?"

"I can't tell you Phil. I wish I could."

I got up in a daze and started to walk out.

"Phil, she really liked you a lot. She always seemed so happy when she was with you," Jean said as I walked out.

Later on that night everyone was sacked out, except Clock. He wasn't back yet. I laid on my bunk feeling pretty sorry for myself, trying to figure out why.

Clock finally came in and sat down on his bunk. Taking off his shoes he asked, "You still awake, Kuni?"

"Yeah."

"Jean told me what happened."

"For Christ sake, Clock, if you tell me you're sorry I'll climb out of this bed and jump all over you."

"Well, then go to hell, you little shit," Clock replied. "I really am sorry, though. What happened? I thought you two were getting along great."

"I don't know, Clock. She just said she didn't want to see me again."

"Jean likes you, and she felt real bad about telling you."

"I don't know how you two ever found girlfriends. You guys don't know a damn thing about women," Paul said as he sat up in his bed.

"What the hell do you mean by that?" I asked.

"Well, it's pretty damn obvious why she doesn't want to see you again," he said.

"If you know so damn much about women, why doesn't she want to see me again?"

"She doesn't want to see you get your head bashed in," I looked at Paul with a dumb expression on my face as he went on. "She is afraid her brother is going to beat the hell out of you the next time he drinks. So she figures if she stays away from you her brother will also. And I agree with her. Let's face it, the guy hates you. Actually, I think he would hate anyone that dates his sister, but you not being Jewish is all the more reason."

"I have noticed that he has taken quite a dislike for me and, Paul, I just can't understand it. Usually my splendid charm and humorous wit wins everyone over," I said as Paul threw a pillow at me.

"I'm not kidding, Kuni. I think you better give it some thought about staying away from her," Paul said.

"I've just given it some thought, and I'm not going to take it. I'm going after her, and I don't give a shit what that guy thinks or what he does to me."

"I think you're nuts. Which is why I knew you were going to say that," Paul said. "If that's the way you want it, go ahead, but if he starts crowding you, let me know and I'll see if I can take him off your back. Now I wish the two of you would shut up so I can go back to sleep."

I laid back and thought that at least she still likes me.

That weekend we started our war on the guests. I really didn't contribute much to our little skirmish. I was too busy trying to figure a way to get Naomi to talk to me. Clock and Ed went around and loosened the lids on the salt, pepper and sugar containers.

We began to reap our spoils. We started getting back cups of coffee full of sugar and plates covered with salt or pepper.

When our boss confronted us with all of our evil deeds,

we accepted our fate and only did the right thing. We blamed the busboys. Regardless of all of this, nothing had changed and the poor busboys were getting all the hell from the boss and the guests.

After getting back to our bunks at 10 o'clock Sunday night, we decided we had to hold another council of war and map out our next course of action.

Alas, those poor guests were finished. After our council of war, even we were feeling sorry for them. I got so wrapped up in our plans, it took my mind completely off the troubles I was having with Naomi. I liked it that much.

Lats, of course, was against the whole idea and said he would wash his hands of the whole matter. In fact, he went so far as to take a shower to wash his whole body of it. He left, mumbling something about us being crazy, sadistic, and perverted as the rest of us sat around my bunk in the corner chuckling.

The next morning we went to work tired and beat. But, if the people looked at us closer, they would have seen the contented smile and probably a guy in red with a tail and pitchfork in our eyes. That is, all except Lats, he had pure terror in his.

Our whole plan centered on Paul and his apron. Paul was the slopper. His job was to slop the extra food off the dishes and rack them.

Seeing as how Paul was as delicate and dainty as a gorilla attending a women's club tea party, his apron usually got pretty sloppy. Whenever we were finished, he would put his apron through the machine to clean it. In keeping to our plan, he stopped doing that. After the breakfast and dinner dishes, Paul just rolled up his apron and hid it under the dishwasher.

Since I wasn't having any luck talking to Naomi, I decided to write her a note. Clock was dishing out the dessert, so I figured that would be the best way of getting the note to her. I wrote a note saying that I missed her, and I had to talk to her. I slipped it under a piece of cake and then realized that I forgot to name a place to meet. Writing another note asking her to meet me by the piano in the gym, I put that under the other side of the cake.

"Jim, make sure Naomi gets this piece of cake," I said when I grabbed the busboy that covers her table.

I figured she would see the note right away, but she was too busy talking to a friend of hers. She took a fork full of cake along with my note and stuck it in her mouth.

This is not going right, I said to myself as she was fishing the stupid paper out of her mouth. After she unfolded and read it, she looked up with a real dumb expression on her face. She stopped Jim as he went by and whispered something to him. As Jim was coming over to me those little kids were thinking this was something exciting and they were giggling over it. Stupid kids.

"Naomi doesn't know what you mean by the 'P.S.'," Jim said when he got over to me.

"Oh. Shit! She got the second note first. Tell her to read the other note first."

After Jim told her to read the other note, I stood there by the door as Naomi was breaking up her cake looking for the other note. Those stupid little kids were giggling behind their hands and pointing to the door where I stood. I thought, *You dumb little brats. There's got to be an easier way of doing this*.

Finally she found the note and read it. Looking up she shook her head "no" a few times and got up and left in a hurry.

"Ah, shit," I said as I went back to the dishes.

"Give up on her Kuni," Paul said to me, as I got back, "It wasn't meant to be. The both of you are only being hurt by it."

"I can't, Paul. I love her."

He shook his head and went back to work. That night I went up to the gym and waited by the piano until they were getting ready to close up.

"She's not going to come, Kuni," Clock said as he stopped by. "Come on, I'll walk back to the shack with you."

After supper the next night the campers went to some kind of Jewish services. When I got finished with work I took that opportunity to devise some way of getting Naomi to talk to me. I gathered up some stuff and went over to her cabin. Climbing up to the backside of the roof, I waited for them to get back.

When they came back I wrote a little note to Naomi asking her to come to the back window and talk to me. I tied the note to a rock with a string and lowered the string down the chimney of their fireplace. To get their attention, I dropped another rock down. With that, there came a little bit of scrambling going on. I felt someone take the note off the rock. After what seemed to be a long time, I felt a jerk on the string and pulled the rock back up. Naomi had asked me to come to the back window. I scrambled down and looked over the edge.

"You're crazy," she said as she leaned out the window.

"Yes, I am," I answered.

"Would you please get down off the roof?"

"No, not until you agree to meet me somewhere and talk to me."

"Please, Phil, you're going to get in trouble when the counselor comes."

"Nope, I'm not leaving until you agree to talk to me. You either meet me somewhere or explain why my skeleton is on your roof."

"Phil, you are being very childish. You are going to get the other girls in trouble."

I didn't think the other girls were that worried about it. They were giggling and telling her to meet me. "Naomi, I'm sorry about that, but I have to see you and talk to you one more time."

"Phil, please, it's hard enough. Don't make it harder on me."

"Naomi, how hard do you think it is for me? Meet me this once and then if this is what you really want, I'll leave you alone and won't bother you again."

She went back inside and was talking to Jean while I just sat there. "Phil," she said as she stuck her head out the window again. "I'll meet you at our place."

I went and got a blanket to sit on in the back of the truck. What was I going to say to make her see me again? Maybe I should have thought this out better.

"I didn't think you were coming," I said, when she finally got there.

"I was trying to find a way to explain things to you."

"Did you find a way?"

"No."

"Why don't you just tell me what happened? I must have missed something somewhere along the way cause I thought things were going okay with us."

"Phil, it's not you."

"Is it your brother?"

"Yes," she said, pausing for a moment. "You don't know him like I do. He drinks too much, and he gets mean when he is like that."

"Why? Why would you seeing me bother him that much?"

"Please don't blame him, Phil. It's not his fault, it's mine. Oh God, Phil," she continued. "I never wanted to tell you this because I know you are going to hate me."

I reached over and took her hands in mine and she squeezed them tight as tears started to roll down her face.

"Phil, I was forced to come to camp this summer. About two weeks before I came here I had an abortion," she sobbed. "My parents sent me up here so no one would find out."

Boy, that sure took the wind out of me. Just to show you how smart I am about women, I thought she was still a virgin. "How did it happen?" I asked when I was able to speak again. "No, I take that back. It doesn't matter to me, that should be your own business."

"See, I knew you would hate me," she said, crying.

I took her by the shoulders and kissed each cheek where the tears came down.

"Naomi, I am falling in love with you. It bothers me that you were hurt like that, but it doesn't change the way I feel about you one bit."

She looked up at me and smiled a little, and this time I kissed her right.

"Phil, I met this boy back home and I thought we were both in love."

I kissed her again to stop her. "Naomi, you don't have to tell me the story. It doesn't matter.

"No, Phil I have to. I want you to know how it was and that there isn't anything left between us. It happened. I wouldn't make any excuses for that. When I found out I was pregnant, he wasn't too happy about that, but we decided to tell my parents. Well, the boy wasn't Jewish and Dad told the boy that marriage was out of the question. Dad brought up the idea of an abortion, and he was all for it. He was glad to be relieved of it. I sat there and they never asked me what I wanted," she continued to cry again. "They just talked like it was an accident and it was just another case he was settling out of court for one of his clients. Nobody cared what I wanted. They talked like I wasn't there. I felt so dirty and ashamed."

She was really crying hard now. I held her in my arms and let her cry it out.

"When my brother found out," she started again after a while, "he wanted to get the boy and kill him. But by this time everything was settled, and the boy was gone. I'm afraid my brother might take it out on you. Phil, I have hurt so many people. I don't think I could bear seeing you get hurt too. I hurt my parents, myself, you but most of all I hurt my little baby. They wouldn't even tell me if I had a little girl or a little boy."

I wrapped my arms around her real tight and held on to her, and she cried and sobbed and her whole body shook. I don't know how long I held on to her, but it seemed like forever. After a while she pulled away and touched my face, kissed me, and said "Phil, I love you."

"Naomi, I wish I knew the right words to say to take your pain and sadness away, I just know that I love you."

"Phil, you said all the right things when you held on to me, Your heart was talking to my heart all the time you were holding me."

I walked her back to her cabin, and we talked, and kissed, and held hands, and kissed and just held on to one another, not really wanting to let go.

Walking back to my shack, I knew that tonight I felt something for another person that I never thought existed.

Opening up the door I turned the light on and went around and woke everyone up. I didn't even mind all the swear words I was hearing.

"Ok, you guys, I need to talk."

They all sat up bitching and complaining. Finally Clock said, "Ok Kuni, what's up?

So I told them all that we got back together, but I left out all the stuff about the abortion part. No one said a word while I told them. They all gave me their advice which boiled down to no matter what I did, they had my back. I said I was not going to stop seeing Naomi no matter what, her brother could beat me all he wants but I will not stop seeing her.

"Kuni,," Paul said, "Life was a lot easier when we were too stupid to have emotions. Besides, he better not beat on my little buddy."

"I just wanted to tell you guys that I think you're all great. In fact the whole world is great."

"Are you drunk?" Lats asked.

"No, he isn't," Paul laughed. "He's back together with Naomi, and he's in love."

"Oh shit," Ed said. "I liked it better when he just moped around."

"Kuni, be careful," Paul said, "I know both of you are in love, but you two are from different worlds, and the end of camp is coming soon. This will not end well."

"Paul, we can make this work out. I know we can. It has to."

CHAPTER SIXTEEN

As the week went by, Naomi and I spent as much time together as we could squeeze in. We had decided to keep it as much of a secret as possible. I didn't like that too much, but hey, as long as I got to see her. Did I mention that I was on cloud nine? I didn't even mind our sacrifices in the line of duty with our war on the guests. Even though our sacrifices were great. Our battle plan was coming along excellently. In fact, our hopes for an ultimate victory were high.

The week started without incident. Paul continued to roll up his apron after each meal and hid it under the counter. By the middle of the week Paul, Ed, and I were taking turns running to the window to get fresh air. Lats and Clock were lucky they were far enough away. Soon enough, though, our fellow workers were beginning to stop and look around when they walked by our area. The busboys started commenting on the smell whenever they dropped dishes off. Paul always told them there was no smell. If they continued to insist there was, Paul would growl at them and tell them once more. Usually that would convince them that everything smelled great. The rest of the kitchen help noticed how upset Paul became on that subject of the smell. So they kept their distance. They didn't want to upset Paul, but mainly it was because of the smell. Lats came over periodically to plead with Paul not to go through with it.

But I must give credit where credit is due. Paul handled himself magnificently and with devotion above and beyond the call of duty. Each meal he would slowly unroll his apron, trying not to look at it and then put it on. It was sickening. All the scraps and junk were building up on it, and the smell was getting worse and worse.

Towards the end of the week, Paul had stopped eating altogether. He had turned a light shade of green, and his knees would buckle once in a while. We took turns helping him over to the window. But like a true member of the gang, he stuck it out.

Saturday night finally arrived. By this time everyone in the kitchen was starting to get sick. The apron stunk to high heaven. The moment of truth was upon us. I guess along with the smell. It was time to see if all of our sacrifices would pay off. We waited till after the guests were finished with their dinners. While they were eating dessert and drinking coffee, our plan went into effect. Paul spilled a little more food on his apron for effect. Lats came over to state his case one more time, but Paul wasn't about to let that whole week of suffering go by for nothing. Paul slowly walked over to the dining room, stopping only once to hold on to something. At the door he straightened himself up and took a bus cart for the dirty dishes. Using the cart to help steady himself, he walked in the dining room. We all rushed over to the door to watch as our sadistic and perverted plan unfolded.

Paul went to the first table and stood behind a lady as she talked to her husband. Her first reaction was to stop talking and give her husband a dirty look. He, in turn, told her that she should take more baths in the summer. They both noticed Paul when he reached over the lady to take the dirty dishes off the table. Leaning over with the apron practically in the lady's face, he asked them if they enjoyed the meal. The husband nodded "yes" as he was trying to avoid looking at the apron. The lady was pushing her chair back trying to get away from Paul. She frantically searched for her purse, and when she found it, she jumped up to leave.

"Don't you want your cake and ice cream?" Paul asked the lady while he picked it up to give it to her.

"No, I don't believe so," she answered, backing up so fast that she knocked over the chair.

"You should eat it now, the ice cream is melting all over the cake," Paul commented as he followed her, sticking the plate under her nose.

She looked at the apron and then the cake with the ice cream melting all over it. Cupping her hand over her mouth, she turned and bolted out of the room. Paul turned to the husband, but he was already on his way out.

By this time Paul was beginning to be noticed as he went from table to table. The parents were hurrying to leave before Paul and his apron got there. Eventually our boss Ruth got the word, and she came storming up to Paul. Ruth started to say something but couldn't quite get the words out. Paul gave her that sheepish, hurt look and said, "Why is everyone leaving? I thought the cake was pretty good myself."

Our boss managed to blurt out something about wanting to see us in the office the next morning. Then she proceeded to run out.

When Paul came back in the kitchen, we were rolling around on the floor in hysterics. We ran that apron through the machine six times before we could get it cleaned, but we never could get the smell out. Lats finally put it in bleach water to soak overnight.

When we got back to the shack, we were still smiling about the apron.

"You guys owe me big time for this night," Paul said.

"We are going to get fired for this," Lats said, "I've never been fired from anything in my whole life."

"Lats, see how you learn all these new things by hanging out with us," Ed answered.

"Hell, I should have listened to my teachers when they told me that hanging out with guys would destroy some of my brain cells."

"Don't worry Lats, you have plenty to spare," I said "I will give you some of mine, if you need any."

"Kuni, you don't have any."

We got back to talking about tonight and we all agreed that Paul was a great leader. But I think we all knew that the plan was formed in Clock's dark twisted mind.

That night we didn't get to sleep until four o'clock in the morning. We tried to sleep but someone would laugh and that would set the rest of us to laughing. Lats was worrying about being fired. The rest of us literally laughed ourselves to sleep.

The next morning we were sitting in front of Ruth. Of course, we were shocked to hear what happened last night. Poor Paul was hurt and dejected to learn that he had offended someone. Ruth didn't know what to say, she was trying to find some way to yell at us but didn't know how to do it. She told us that we were not to stay and clear off the guest tables anymore. She agreed that we could do them in the morning. I think the guests told her they never wanted to see us again. Just before we left Ruth did suggest we wash that apron more frequently.

The next day after supper dishes I took my shower, and went up to the canteen hoping to see Naomi. When I walked into the barn, she was sitting upstairs at the piano.

"I was hoping you would come by tonight. Can we go sit in the back of the truck?" Naomi asked.

"Sure, is it because your brother is around?"

"Yes, and he is drinking. Please, please, I don't want any trouble between you two. Please, Phil, for me."

"Naomi, you know I would do anything for you."

We decided to walk down to Paul's truck and when we got there, I realized that I was beginning to love that truck as much as Naomi does.

"Phil, I'm sorry I act so crazy. I know you must think I am weird along with being crazy."

"Naomi, sometimes weird is good, but if you don't know by now how I feel about you, that would be crazy."

"I know I'm not as skinny and pretty as the rest of the girls. Most of the time guys look at me as the third or fourth pick, but when I am with you it is like you only see me."

"You are all I want to see."

After I said that she hugged me and started kissing me. So we sat there and made out until it was time for her to go in. I don't understand why it is so hard to say good night.

When I got back to our shack, everyone but Lats was back. Alice had picked Lats up to go to a movie. Ed was laying down trying to sleep, Paul was cleaning up from working on his truck, and Clock was reading some letters that the girls from home sent him.

"Are those stupid girls still writing to you?" I asked.

"Kuni, you're just jealous."

"Damn right I am, but right now I am seeing the best one of the lot."

"Kuni, you're right. Naomi is a sweetheart. She is Jean's best friend, and Jean says she really likes you. So don't screw it up. We all know what a screw up you are."

Lats walked in just then and started telling us about the movie they saw.

"Who the hell cares about the movie?" Ed said as he sat up in bed, "if you watch any part of the movie you're not doing it right. We want to know how you and Alice made out."

"Shut up Ed," Lats answered. "But Alice did say that Sunday they are having homemade ice cream and pie at the farm. We are all invited. Girlfriends, too, if you want. They also have a swimming pond so we can bring bathing suits if we want to swim."

"Can we just go skinning dipping?" I asked.

"That is exactly what Alice said you were going to say, and she said the answer is NO."

"Clock, are you thinking what I'm thinking? I said.

"Kuni, as always I am way ahead of you. Sunday is an open day for the campers. Let's try to talk them into going up to the farm with us."

"Lats," I said, "make sure you give Alice a big kiss from all of us, unless, of course, she would want me to do it."

The next night we told the girls about going up to the farm for homemade ice cream and cake. We also told them to bring bathing suits so we could swim.

Sunday we did our usual escape route and headed up to the farm. We all sat around on the front porch while Alice and her mom brought out cake and ice cream. The cake and ice cream were a big hit, and we all loved it. Naomi and Jean had all sorts of questions for Alice and her mom, while us guys and Alice's dad talked mostly about the farm. Alice's dad opened up a lot to Paul and me about the farm, and we had a great visit sitting on the porch.

Then we all took turns changing into our bathing suits and went down to the pond. It was a small pond with a dock about 15 feet from shore. Jean, Naomi, Clock and I swam out to the dock and sat around enjoying the sun. The girls were talking about school and hanging out with their friends, shopping, and Clock and I. Clock and I in turn talked about hopping trains, Nick's, shooting rats in the landfill, cars, school sports, and Jean and Naomi. I think the girls went a little nuts when we talked about standing on a bridge and jumping into the coal cars as they went by below us.

"You guys are crazy," Jean and Naomi both said together.

"Yes, we are," Clock and I answered together.

We had a quiet ride back to camp, not wanting the day to end. After everyone left, Naomi and I stayed in the back of the truck.

"Phil, I love you so much. I had a great time. I always have a great time when I am with you. Sometimes I feel so guilty about being so happy."

"What do you mean about feeling guilty?"

"Like sometimes, I feel I don't deserve to be this happy. Never mind, Phil, I'm just going to miss you so much. Promise me that we will keep in touch with each other. I don't want this to be just another summer fling. I want more than that. I want you."

"Naomi, you will always be in my life for you have my heart, and I don't want it back. I love you."

CHAPTER SEVENTEEN

"The biggest problem that Naomi and I have is trying to find a spot to be alone," I complained to Clock as we were walking down to our shack one afternoon.

"Why don't you take a blanket and go over to the baseball field."

"Are you nuts?" I replied. "Half of the camp uses the baseball field to make out."

"You could always use the boathouse. I hear that's a good place to make out in."

"You smart ass," I said, "The way you and Jean always disappear, I know you have a good spot."

"Yeah, I have a really good place to go. No one knows about it, and I want to keep it that way."

"Come on, Clock, you have to tell me. It's the code of the gang. You don't want to break the code."

"Ha, code of the gang. First of all, we don't have a code, and second, we don't have a gang."

"Well, if we had a gang that would be the code. Besides, don't make me beat it out of you."

When Clock finally stopped laughing, he said, "Okay, Kuni, the best way is to show you."

We turned around and started walking back. Instead of

crossing the road to go back up to the main building, we turned and walked over to the laundry building.

"See that window on this side?" Clock said as he nodded to the side of the building away from the camp.

The front of the laundry building faced the gravel road while the right side faced the highway and the rest of the camp. The left side was the side Clock was referring to and that side faced the storage building. The window was located in the area between the laundry and storage building.

"That window is supposed to be nailed shut," Clock added, "but you can pull the nail out and open the window."

"You sneaky bastard. How the hell did you find out about that?" Sometimes I get completely amazed with Clock's ability.

"Oh, I have my ways. It helps if you had a hammer and took it out first," he answered. "Just put that nail back in and no one will know about it."

"Clock, did you know that you are my hero? I want to be just like you when I grow up."

"Screw you, Kuni," Clock said as he flashed me the finger.

My next roadblock was trying to get Naomi to crawl through that window with me. I just knew she would say, "Are you nuts?" That night I told Naomi about the window in the laundry building.

"Well, it's about time you found some place where we can be alone."

We very nonchalantly managed to stroll over to the parking lot. From there we snuck across the gravel road and between the storage and laundry buildings.

"Are you scared?" Naomi asked.

"Yes. A little. How about you?"

"I'm petrified."

"Do you want to go back?" I asked.

"No, I waited long enough to be alone with you. Besides, it's kind of exciting. I've never broken into a building before."

I pulled the nail out and quietly opened the window. It didn't make a sound. That Clock, I bet he even oiled the window.

"Here, I'll help you up," I said.

"Not on your life! You go first," Naomi replied.

Women, I thought as I climbed in the window. I reached down and pulled Naomi up and helped her in.

"It's dark in here," Naomi said as she squeezed my hand.

Boy, she was right. I couldn't see anything. We stumbled around and found a corner to sit in.

"I feel like we are breaking the law or something," Naomi said.

"Oh, that's just because I'm such an exciting guy."

"Ha!" Naomi laughed. "Weird would be a better word. I never know what to expect from you."

"My little chickadee," I said in my best W. C. Fields imitation. "I would tell you of your beauty. That is, if I was able to see you."

"Oh, stop that now," Naomi said.

"Okay, here's looking at you kid," I went to my Bogart. Boy, I was on a roll. "You must remember this, a kiss is just a kiss."

"Stop it!" she said.

"It's no good kid. We just can't go on meeting like this," I went on. "One of these days you're going to want more than just all this dirty laundry," I waved my arm around. "You'll get tired of me and go off to find someone who owns a laundromat."

"You're crazy," Naomi laughed and slid into my arms.

We were having a nice time being alone and while I was kissing Naomi, she gasped. "Phil, there's someone outside the window!" she whispered real low. Shit, here I thought it was because I was such a good kisser. I turned around and saw a couple of shadows out there.

"Is that Clock and Jean?" Naomi asked.

"No," I whispered. "Clock said he wouldn't come here tonight."

"Well, who could it be?"

"I don't know. Follow me." I grabbed her hand and we crawled to the doorway and went around the corner into the next room.

"I'm scared!" Naomi said as one of them opened the window.

It looked like a shadow of a girl that climbed in first, followed by a guy.

"See," I whispered right into her ear, "she went first."

She stuck her hand over my mouth and told me to shut up.

There was a lot of giggling going on while they were getting settled down.

"What do we do?" Naomi asked.

"It looks like we have to stay here till they leave."

We sat there and listened as they were talking. I was getting embarrassed because boy was it getting raunchy, and with that the clothes were coming off.

"You men are all thumbs. Let me get that." The girl said. I sort of snickered at that and got a poke in the ribs.

"Oh! Benny, you love me, don't you?" she said again. "Tell me you do."

"Oh yeah, baby," he groaned. "I love you, I love you."

I snickered again and Naomi stuck her mouth up to my ear. "Don't you dare laugh out loud," she pleaded.

"Oh," the girl moaned. "You're so, so masculine."

The next thing I knew Naomi had one hand clamped over my mouth and the other one on the back of my head. She was squeezing like mad. The only problem with that was, she also had her hand over my nose. I had a hard time trying to pull her hand away. She was hanging on for her dear little life.

We sat in the next room huddled together listening to obscene oh's and ah's.

I put my mouth to Naomi's ear. "I wish we could record this." This time she put her hand over her mouth.

Finally, what seemed like forever, they got everything put back together and left.

After they had plenty of time to get away I breathed a sigh of relief. Then I started laughing and that started Naomi giggling.

"I feel terrible for those poor kids. We intruded on their privacy," Naomi said.

"Hey, we were here first. It seems like it was the other way around."

"Yes," she answered, "but they didn't know we were here."

"Well, I could tell them," I said.

"Don't you dare! I would just die from embarrassment if those kids knew I was here."

"Relax, they didn't know we were here. Besides, I don't even know who they were. I know one thing. They were not kids. They were probably counselors."

"They were," Naomi replied.

"You know them? Who were they?" I asked.

"I don't know who the guy was, but I think I know the girl. And I am not going to tell you."

"Oh, come on," I pouted.

"No, and let's get out of here before someone else comes. I don't think I could sit through that again."

"Yeah, you're right," I said. "So much for Clock's spot that no one else knows about."

We climbed out of the window and worked our way back to the parking lot.

"The hell with this. Come on." I said. We went across the parking lot and down to the shack.

"Is everyone decent?" I said as I stuck my head in the door.

"Quick, hide her under the bed," Ed yelled.

"Come on," I said as I took Naomi's hand.

"But!"

"Don't listen to Ed. There's no girl. Ed is just nuts."

"Hi, Naomi," Paul and Ed said as we walked in.

"How come you hang around that guy when I'm available?" Ed added.

"You're not available. What about that girl under your bed?" she answered.

"Paul, how 'bout letting me use your truck?" I asked while I grabbed a blanket.

"Okay," he said as he tossed the keys over to me. "Don't use up all the gas."

"Just what are you up to?" Naomi asked as we walked over to the truck.

"Nothing! We are just going to be alone for a while,"

We got in Paul's truck and I turned to Naomi, "Do you just want to sit and talk or go somewhere and neck?" *Boy, now, that's class. Hell, there must be a better way to phrase that*, I thought.

Naomi laughed, "We can talk any time. I think we should go and neck."

I couldn't believe she agreed to necking. Wow, what a girl! Reverse was hard to find in Paul's truck, but I finally found it. I looked out the back window and stepped on the gas but nothing happened.

"You have to start the truck first, Phil,"

Damn, she would have to notice that. "Oh!" I turned the key and the truck jerked backwards. Whoops! "I'm sorry, I wanted to hurry up before you changed your mind," I said.

"Don't worry," Naomi smiled and squeezed my hand. "I wouldn't change my mind."

Boy, do I love this girl, I thought as I leaned over and kissed her. After I got the truck started, I backed up, deliberately sweeping the baseball field with the headlights. We were greeted by a lot of swearing.

"Such language," I said. "Why do I think those boys should be ashamed of themselves?"

"You know you're rotten, don't you?" Naomi laughed.

Rather than going up to the highway, I went the other way on the dirt road. That way led us past our shack up to the pastures of the neighboring farm; I drove about a mile and found what looked like a nice pasture. Don't ask me how I could tell a nice pasture in the dark. I was just trying to find the first available place to stop. We climbed over the fence, and I spread the blanket out being careful not to hit a cow pie.

"It's a nice night. I like it here," Naomi said as she snuggled up to me. We laid there just talking mostly and kissing once in a while. After a while we laid there kissing mostly and talking once in a while. I didn't know that lying on a blanket looking at the stars could be so romantic. I don't remember when we stopped talking and started to neck. Somewhere along the way we went past the talking part.

Normally I let my hands wander until she stopped me. It's like a game, I guess. I would then pretend to be sad and rejected, but in reality I was usually glad.

Well, I kept waiting for her to stop me, but she wasn't saying anything. I had already gone further than I ever did before, and if I didn't know what to do, I sure as hell wanted to find out.

I was halfway lying on top of Naomi, really getting involved with the whole affair when she let off with a scream. I was kissing her on the neck and it damn near broke my eardrum.

"What! What the hell's wrong?" I yelled as I jerked up wondering what happened to her.

Naomi was pulling up her blouse and staring past me, I spun around and a stupid cow stood there slobbering on me.

"It's just a cow," I said as I tried to get my breath back and my heart to beat normally. "What are you trying to do, scare the hell out of me?" I asked.

"Please, Phil, get that thing out of here, make it go away." Naomi pleaded. Her poor little heart must have been beating twice as fast. She was just shaking like crazy.

"Get out of here, you stupid cow." I slapped it on the rump. *Boy, talk about dumb animals*, I thought. I chased it away but it only went twenty feet and stopped.

To hell with that cow, I thought as I went back to Naomi. I held on to Naomi until she calmed down a little.

"When I opened my eyes that thing was staring right down at me. I didn't know what it was," Naomi finally said.

"I never thought I'd see the day when a cow ruined my love life. I'm going to wait till that cow gets together with a bull and then I am going to go over and stare at them. Do you think that will work?"

"No," she laughed. "I bet they wouldn't care."

"Where did you learn to scream like that? God, I had visions of some madman with an ax coming down on us," I said.

"You sure did jump pretty fast."

"Well, that damn cow probably will leave an emotional scar on my ability to fool around from now on. Normal people, when they are necking, don't keep looking over their shoulder for a stupid cow," I replied.

"Oh, I don't think it will have any effect on your ability to make out. Besides," she said, getting serious, "it only ruined your love life for one night."

After I left Naomi at her cabin, I kept thinking of what she said. It dawned on me that we came pretty close to going all the way. Back in my bed I laid awake for some time. Tonight was not like the other nights, and I was a little scared. I think we reached a point where we would have gone all the way. That was something I hadn't expected. If we did go all the way, there would have been the chance that she might get pregnant. She went through hell with her parents when she got pregnant before. God, I couldn't let her go through that again. She was probably counting on me to have some protection. But I didn't. Boy, I really could have screwed things up. Holy shit, that cow sure saved us. Maybe I shouldn't eat hamburgers any more.

I finally fell asleep with a determination that I was going to get some rubbers. I didn't know if I would get that close again, but if I did I wanted to have some protection for her. Stupid cow.

Saturday after dinner dishes, I asked Paul if he was going into town.

"Well, I guess I could pick up some things. Did you want to get anything?"

"Yeah, I wanted to pick up a few things, too," I answered.

On the way in I suddenly realized what I wanted to do when I met Naomi tomorrow night.

"Paul, what kind of wine would be good to drink when you are just sitting around talking. I mean a special wine, like for a picnic or something?"

"Well, brandy is a good drink."

"Do you think you could run in the store and get me some?"

"Sure I could, Kuni, but brandy is expensive."

"The hell with the expense," I said, "Can you buy me half a pint of it?"

I don't know what the hell he started laughing about.

Paul went in and bought me a whole pint of brandy. We picked up the rest of the stuff he wanted. As we were getting ready to leave, I asked Paul if he could stop at the drugstore.

Paul looked at me strangely, "Kuni, are you sure about this?"

"Sure about what?"

"You know damn well what I mean. At least you're smart enough to get some rubbers, right?"

"Yeah, that's why I want to stop here."

"Kuni, do you want me to go in with you?" Paul asked.

"No, that's alright. I'll be right back."

There was an older woman who looked like she was close to thirty waiting on customers. Just before she got to me, a lady came in and started looking around.

"What can I do for you?" the woman asked.

Oh, God! I can't ask for them in front of her. "This lady was first," I said.

"No," she replied. "You were here first."

For Christ sake, lady. I thought. "No, you were first. Go ahead."

"No, you were getting ready when I came up to the counter."

"I want to look around some more," I said. *Geez, why do these things happen to me?*

While she waited on her another lady came in. This one looked like she could be my grandmother. *Where the hell are all these ladies coming from?*

She looked over at me, and I told her I was still looking. After both ladies left, I went up to the counter.

"Now what can I get you?" she asked.

"Oh, ah, let me, ah, have, ah, pack of gum." I stumbled around.

I took the gum and left. "Christ, a pack of gum, you idiot! You blooming idiot!" I kept saying as I walked out to the truck.

"Well, did you get what you wanted?" Paul asked.

"No, I'll be right back," I said as I went back in.

I came back swearing at myself. "For Christ sake! A roll of Life Savers, you idiot, you blooming idiot."

"Kuni, do you want me to go in and get them?" Paul asked.

"Bullshit, Paul, if I can be man enough to use them, I should be man enough to buy them," I answered as I went back in.

That woman was still behind the counter, so I gathered up all the nerve I could and walked up to her. *Courage*, I thought, *that's all you need. Come right out and ask for them like a man.*

"My brother wanted me to buy something here," I said.

"Does he want you to buy some prophylactics?" she asked with a stupid grin on her face.

"No, he wanted me to buy a pack of rubbers," I answered.

She shook her head a little and reached down below the counter and gave me a pack.

"Did you get them?" Paul asked.

"Yeah."

"Kuni, let's stop for a coke, I'll buy."

"Sure, Paul, but I'll do the buying."

"Kuni," Paul finally said as we sat drinking our cokes, "I probably know a little more about this than you, so if you have any questions all you have to do is ask."

"Paul, you've gone all the way with a girl, right?"

"Yeah, I did."

"What was it like afterwards, I mean was it the same as before? Did you both feel the same about each other afterwards?"

"No Kuni, it's not the same, everything changes afterwards. If there is a deep feeling between the two of you, then it will be more so afterwards. If not, then it will be worse. Do you know what I am saying?"

"I think so," I answered. We were both silent for a while.

"Kuni, it will be ok. You were right in getting the rubbers. You want her to remember it, not regret it. This will probably be your first time, so don't be an asshole. It's just not about you. You won't do everything right, so just be yourself. God, no, don't be yourself, be like your Bogart. Let me give you one last piece of advice, when you both are finished, hold on to her tight and tell her you love her. Hold her as long as you can, and let her know how much she means to you. This is important."

"Paul, thanks, you're one hell of a friend, you know that?"

"Yeah, someone has to take care of you assholes."

CHAPTER EIGHTEEN

Naomi and I planned to meet tonight after their church services. By the time we got finished with the supper dishes, and I went to take a shower and dress, she would be ready to go. I liked this night of the week because the campers are allowed to stay up later on this night after services.

Paul agreed to let me use his truck. This time I didn't have to convince him too much. I took all day getting ready for my date with Naomi. That took a lot of convincing with Clock and a few of the chefs. After using all my charms, I finally gathered up the things I would need for tonight.

After the supper dishes, I took a shower, got dressed, and by the time I met Naomi, it was already dark. She had ducked down so no one would see her in the truck with me. I drove back past the baseball field and up the same gravel road we went up a couple of nights ago. I drove a little ways until I found a field that had no cows. Stupid cows!

"What are you up to?" Naomi asked.

"Well, I've decided that since it's such a nice day, we should go on a picnic."

"A picnic!" she replied. "It's dark out here."

"I was hoping you wouldn't notice that. Besides, you can't expect everything to be perfect, can you?"

"You're crazy."

"Yes, I am. Besides, why do people keep saying that to me? Lots of people go on picnics. Don't you want to have a picnic with the hero that saved you from that terrible cow?" I asked.

"I wouldn't miss this for anything," she laughed.

I pulled the truck off to the side of the road and shut it off. We got out and walked to the back of the truck.

"Here, you can carry this," I said as I gave Naomi the blanket. There was a basket left, and I took it.

"You crazy nut. You really are serious about this picnic," Naomi said.

"Of course, I don't see anything strange about this."

"No, you wouldn't," Naomi laughed.

We went through the fence and found a nice flat spot to spread out our blanket.

"What do you have in that basket?" Naomi asked.

"Stuff for a picnic. What do you think?"

"With you, I never know," she said.

We both sat down on the blanket and Naomi said, "Well, what now?"

"Well, as you know," I answered. "I usually do things differently." That must have struck her as funny because it set her to giggling, "Now, you've heard of a candle light dinner," I went on, "so I thought, hell, why not have a candlelight picnic?"

With that I pulled a couple of candles and a candle holder out of the basket. I lit a candle as she went from giggling to laughing. I took out a couple of paper plates, gave one to Naomi, and passed her a few napkins.

"Now, what good is a picnic without some cold fried chicken?" I said as I pulled out two pieces of chicken and a bag of chips.

"You know, I really think you're nuts, but you're oh, so adorable" Naomi said as we sat, eating our chicken and chips.

"Now you have to admit that this picnic has style," I replied in my Bogart mode. "Look kid, you stick with me and we'll go first class all the way. Nothing but the best for you."

When Naomi was finally able to speak after choking, "You sure do have style. I don't think I'll ever have a picnic to compare with this one again," Naomi said.

"Something is missing," I said when we finished up our chicken and chips. I reached into the basket and brought out a jar. "I know what it is. We don't have any ants. What's a picnic without ants." I continued as I took off the lid to the jar. "Don't worry, I even thought of that. I brought my own." I said as I started shaking out the jar over her lap.

Naomi jumped up yelling and trying to brush off her shorts.

"I'm sorry," I said laughing. "There wasn't anything in the jar. Honest."

I was still laughing when she jumped on me. We wrestled around on the blanket while she kept trying to tickle me. I found out that she was a lot more ticklish than me. Then something happened. She stopped horsing around with me, and she was just holding on to me as tight as she could.

"I love you, Phil, my heart will always be your home," She whispered in my ear.

I cupped her face in my hands and kissed the tear in her eye. "I love you, Naomi."

We lay there together and it seemed to me that the rest of the world just went away. The worries and fears that I thought I would have were gone.

"I want to," she whispered in my ear,

"Naomi, I have to tell you this is the first time for, well, you know," I told her.

"Phil it's ok, really. This is my first time with someone I love so much," she answered.

We slowly undressed each other and I was a little embarrassed when she helped me with the rubber. So much for doing everything right.

With the candle flickering we lay on the blanket and made love to one another.

Naomi and I just lay in each other's arms with the blanket wrapped around us to keep warm. Neither one of us said anything for a long while; I just wanted to lay there with her in my arms forever.

"The candle is burned out," Naomi finally said.

"So am I," I answered. "Ouch!" she smacked me in the ribs and then grabbed the blanket to cover back up.

"Phil, I wish I could make time stand still for this minute. I've never been happier than right now."

"This will last forever for me because I will remember tonight until I die," I said.

I reached out of the blanket and lit the other candle. We hugged each other and watched the candle burn.

"Phil, you don't realize how much your tenderness and love means to me right now," Naomi finally said.

"Huh? What do you mean?"

"Nothing, let's just say that you answered one of my prayers."

"And you say I'm strange," I replied somewhat confused.

"Well, you are a little strange," she laughed, "but you're just right."

"Ok, first you say I am strange, then you say I am just right. Explain yourself."

"Phil, we are sitting in the middle of a pasture, on a blanket, having a candlelight picnic, completely naked and we just made love to one another. We can't get much stranger than that, but right now for me it is just right. It's perfect."

This time I laughed. "I was right, you are just as strange as I am. But you mentioned one thing, we are just sitting here." I reached in the basket and pulled out two sticks. "This one is yours."

"What's this for?"

"These are to toast marshmallows with."

"Marshmallows!"

"Yeah, hey, stick with me, kid. I told you I always go first class," I said as I gave Naomi a couple marshmallows. I only could get four.

As we toasted our marshmallows over the candle, I could tell she was impressed with my debonair, man-of-the-world ways.

"I know what you're thinking," I said.

"What am I thinking?"

"I bet you're thinking, sure this guy can really have a picnic with style and class but what can he do for an encore? Well, now, marshmallows toasted over a candle flame would be enough for any ordinary person, but not this kid. I figured you deserve more than just something ordinary. I can be just as high class as any big city man-about-town. So to show you that I have style, I bought what everyone should have with marshmallows…wine!"

"Wine!" Naomi said as I took the bottle out of the basket.

"Sure," I answered. "You have wine with fish and meat, why not with marshmallows."

So I poured out our brandy into our paper cups and we drank our brandy wrapped up in our blanket while we lay there looking at the stars. *This has got to be the greatest night of my life*, I said to myself.

"Do you want to bet what I'm thinking now?" Naomi whispered.

"I hope it's the same thing I have on my mind." I answered.

"It is."

Naomi kept her head on my shoulder while I drove back. I parked the truck by our shack and walked Naomi back to her cabin.

"Phil, I had the best time of my life tonight. I'll never forget tonight, and I'll never forget you. I love you."

What a night! I don't think my feet touched the ground all the way back to the shack.

I lay in my bed for a long time thinking, *God, I love that girl*.

CHAPTER NINETEEN

The next Sunday afternoon was the talent contest. Well, it wasn't really a contest because everyone received the same award. It's put on each year for the parents to come up and watch their kids perform on stage. Naomi was to play the piano, and her parents were coming up to watch her perform.

I often told Naomi that our song was "As Time Goes By." So when Naomi was picked to play two songs on the piano she chose "As Time Goes By" as one of her selections.

Practice for all the participants started an hour after supper. Naomi would help out with the younger kids and play the piano for some of the other ones who sang. By that time I would be up in the gym waiting for everyone else to go home. When we were finally alone, I would go up and sit on the stage. I usually kept quiet and didn't say much, just sat and listened. Naomi was in a world of her own when she played her piano. After she played for a while, she would stop and ask me how it was. Hell, she could bang on a tin can and I would think it was great.

After she was finished, we would walk back to our truck—Naomi and I began to call it "our" truck by now. There we would neck and talk. But this week a lot of the times she just laid her head on my chest and clung to me. When she was like that, I just held on to her and told her I loved her.

On Friday night, we were especially somber. Camp would be over two weeks from today, and we didn't want to leave one another. We both promised to write and next summer we would meet again here.

"I'm going to miss you," Naomi cried.

"We said we weren't going to make a big deal about leaving," I said.

"I know, but I can't help it. I am sad about leaving and I'm really, really going to miss you. It's been so good being with you, and when you leave, I'm going to be so lonely again," Naomi said as tears filled her eyes.

"We still have two more weeks," I said as I wiped a tear from her cheek.

"You're right," she said as she tried to smile.

Nevertheless, for some reason, that night was the hardest night of all for us to let go of one another.

I tried to go to sleep that night, but finally gave up and went outside to have a smoke and feel miserable.

"You can't sleep either, huh?" Clock said as he sat beside me.

"I was just sitting here thinking about camp being over in a couple of weeks."

"You really feel bad about leaving her, don't you?" Clock said.

"I don't understand. How could I be so happy one minute and the next I'm miserable?"

"I don't know. Maybe that is what love's supposed to be like."

"How about Jean and you, how will it be like with you two?"

"Oh, I guess it will be a little hard. I like Jean, and we will miss one another a little. She said we'd write, and we probably will for a while. But when school starts we will go back to our friends and gradually it will just fade away to a nice memory of summer."

"I don't know, Clock, like tonight, it was so damn hard to say goodnight. I miss her already, and she isn't gone yet. I don't want to let go of her. It is going to be so hard to say goodbye."

"It will be kind of sad to leave."

"Yeah, it sure will. We had a good summer, didn't we, Clock?"

"It's been a great summer. We had a lot of fun. Before we leave, let's have a real big bash."

"Yeah, sort of like a last hurrah," I answered.

We sat there a little while longer talking of the good times we had here and what we were going to do when we got back to school.

"They say the senior year is always the most fun," I said.

"Yeah," Clock answered. "I am going to try to buckle down more and get better grades. I was serious about going to college later."

"My main goal is to actually graduate," I said. "You know after we graduate everyone is going to go our separate ways, and it is going to be really strange not having you guys around. When all of you leave, I am going to have to grow up. Who is going to tell me how to?"

After gabbing for almost an hour, we called it quits and went to bed. As I lay in bed I thought, hell, Clock was right. It had been a good summer. I had a lot of good times with my friends, and I fell in love with my girl. With that in mind, I finally fell asleep.

Since her parents were there I didn't get to see Naomi at all Saturday.

On Sunday, it was our job to set up the stage for the contest and take it down afterwards. The rest of the guys weren't too happy about that, but I was overjoyed. I got to be close to Naomi again. While everyone was getting ready for the contest, we did manage to smile at one another a few times. Once when I was pushing a table, she came over to help and placed her hand on mine to help me push it in place.

"I'm going to play our song just for you, Phil," She whispered to me as she left.

During the show I stood in the back by the door, hoping no one would chase me away. Naomi came on and played her little heart out. She played something classical first, and it was great. Everyone clapped and cheered. Then she sat back down and played "As Time Goes By," and I swear, it was perfect. No one could have played it better, not even Sam.

With everyone clapping, she stood up and looked around until she saw me. I smiled and winked at her. I sure was proud of her. She winked back at me and smiled as she left the stage.

At the end of the show all the parents and their kids were mingling around the gym floor working their way out.

We were clearing off the stage when Naomi came up to get her music. She stood to the side out of sight of the gym floor and motioned me over.

"It was beautiful, Naomi."

"I played just for you tonight, Phil. I'll see you at the canteen later, ok?"

"I'll be there, I missed you."

"I love you." She said as she reached over and kissed me. Just as she did that her brother came up on the stage.

He came over and grabbed her arm, telling her that her parents were waiting. She went back down the gym floor where her parents were. As she left, he gave me a look of pure hate. He was going to say something to me, but he turned around and left. I turned and saw Paul standing in back of me.

"I don't think he likes me," I said to Paul.

"Be careful, Kuni."

On Sunday night, there were a lot of guests, so we were late getting out. By the time we goofed off at the shack, and I took a shower, it was dark when I left to go up to the canteen. I went across the road and started walking up the path. There were three kids standing around a little way up the path. I didn't think anything of it until I got up to them. About that time Naomi's brother stepped out from among them.

Well, a house doesn't have to fall on me to know when trouble is coming my way. But by that time it was too late for me to go another way. "The hell with it," I thought. "I don't have to go out of my way for him."

"You little bastard. I told you to stay away from my sister," he yelled at me.

I saw then that he was drinking. It was then I decided maybe I could go out of my way for him after all. I was beginning to think that maybe things might not end too well here. Then my smart ass mouth had to kick in, "I don't care what you have to say, You will never stop me from wanting to see Naomi."

"You little bastard, I'm going to make sure you never see her again," he continued.

164

Christ, why does he have to bring up the little part? There's nothing wrong with us small people. He was beginning to get me mad and I don't care who he is, I'm not taking any shit from him.

"Look, I'm not taking any shit from you," I said.

He punched me then. I didn't see it until the last second, and I tried to move, but it caught me right above the eye. The next thing I knew, I was on the ground and my head was beginning to hurt like hell.

Maybe I should rethink that part about not taking any shit from him. I slowly got to my feet while he came strutting over to me.

"I'll teach trash like you to…"

I never let him finish. At that time I hit him somewhere around the mouth with all I had. He backed up more from surprise than anything else. Christ my hand hurt. "Shit," I thought and moved in to hit him again. Now, this will not go down as one of my brighter moments, because as I stepped up to him, he hit me in the stomach.

All the air went out of me as he hit me again. I felt myself getting sick when something hit me on the side of my head. Finding myself on the ground, I decided to take that opportunity to get sick. As I lay there heaving, I thought the bastard must have hit me with a tree. I felt someone pick me up and drag me over to the side of a building and throw me against it. Through the tears I saw Naomi's brother holding me up, hitting me, so I kicked out and heard him yell. As he let go, I fell to the ground.

Laying there listening to him swearing, I tried to smile about that, but it only hurt more. Using the building for support, I tried to stand up but he came at me swinging and hit me all over. I gave up trying to block anything; it was too hard to lift my arms. Things kept fading in and out then. I heard someone arguing and then felt a sharp pain in my side.

The next thing I noticed was the pain. I couldn't see very well and everything was a blur. It was still dark out and I wondered, "What the hell am I doing getting up so early?" As I began to focus, I noticed a tree right in front of me. "Now how the hell did that tree get in here?" and as the rest of the place came into focus, I realized that I wasn't in my bed. "Where the hell am I?"

The pain brought back my memory as I tried to get up. Bad mistake, I sat back down and looked around. There was no one else there. The bastards must have left. Well I don't think I scared them away. God, my head felt like it was going to fall off. Looking down at my shirt, I saw all the blood on it and figured that I must have given him a pretty good fight. Come to think about it, I can only remember him hitting me. When I felt my face, it came to me that all that blood was mine. Boy, I didn't have much to brag about in this fight.

With the tree as support I stood up. My side was hurting, and I was having a hard time breathing. I started up the path when I realized that I couldn't go up to the canteen looking like this. Turning around I stumbled back to the shack. Somewhere on the way back I felt really weak and got sick again.

When I finally got to the shack, I pushed open the door and fell in the shack. Everyone was gathered around me wanting to know what happened. Paul was swearing at Naomi's brother and Lats was looking sick. Meanwhile, Clock and Ed helped me over to my bunk.

"Do I look as bad as I feel?" I asked Clock.

"Worse!"

All of my face hurt, and I could only see out of one eye. And, boy, did my stomach and side hurt. Heaving sure didn't help any. Paul was insisting on taking me up to the camp doctor. I was against that idea but I really didn't think I could fight Paul now.

On the way up there, Ed and Clock wanted to know what happened, but every time I tried to talk, it hurt.

As I sat on the doctor's table he kept mumbling and shaking his head. He started feeling around my head and when he got to my nose I screamed bloody murder.

"What the hell are you doing?" I tried yelling, "Christ, you're hurting me more than he did."

"Well, at least your jaw isn't broken," the doctor said.

He made me take off my shirt and checked out my stomach and side. Then I lay down while he worked on my face for what seemed like forever,

When the doctor finally finished, he opened the door and the rest of the gang came in.

"How is he?" Paul asked.

"Well," the doctor answered, "he's had a pretty bad beating. Besides the obvious bruise marks, his ribs are bruised and he has a broken nose. He also has a concussion so I am going to keep him here for a couple of days."

After the doctor left the room, Paul asked me if Naomi's brother was alone. I told him that there were a couple of guys with him, but he was the only one hitting me.

"I think the other guys pulled him off of me. I remember someone trying to talk him into leaving. That son of a bitch!" I exclaimed, "Now I remember. That bastard kicked me in the side just before he left. No wonder it hurts so much."

"Clock, do you know where those guys hang out?" Paul asked.

The doctor took me upstairs and showed me the room I was to stay in. He chased the rest of the guys out and told me to get some rest. When he left, I went to the bathroom to see if my face looked as bad as it felt. Clock was right, it sure did. I really didn't recognize my face at first. Both eyes were swollen with one completely shut. My nose was taped up and there were bruises all over.

I walked over to the bed and thought, *Shit, I can't sleep tonight. I hurt all over.* I fell asleep as soon as my head hit that pillow.

Chapter Twenty

The nurse came in and woke me up in the morning. I could have done without that. Talk about sore! I felt like I was hit by a bus and dragged a mile, then a herd of wild buffalo trampled me, and I just got run over by the running of the bulls. How they got here from Spain, I don't know. Even with all the pain, when that nurse woke me, I still thought I was looking at the eighth and ninth Wonders of the World. While she opened up the curtains and got me fresh water, I just lay there staring and watching them, I mean her, as she busied herself around the room.

It is amazing that even when a kid's poor body is racked with pain, his mind and body reacts to a beautiful nurse bending over to place a tray of food on his lap. The tray tipped over and nearly spilled the milk.

"Maybe I'll just put this tray on the cart and you can eat whenever you are ready," she said, smiling.

I slid down in the bed and pulled the sheet over my head. She left the room laughing. *Why me, Lord?* I thought, *I'm suffering enough.*

After breakfast, Mrs. Winderberg, our boss, came to see me. "Oh-oh," I thought when she walked in. "This can't be good."

"How do you feel this morning, Philip?" she asked.

"Okay, I guess," I answered, thinking this is really not good.

"You certainly don't look very well. Mr. Pitman is no better off than you are, I'm afraid. Would you care to tell me about the incident?"

"Mr. Pitman?" I asked, puzzled.

"Yes, Richard Pitman. The both of you are suffering from a fist fight. Please, let's not lie and say you don't know anything about it."

Oh, Naomi's brother. It finally came to me. I forgot all about his last name. But all I told Mrs. Winderberg was that I didn't know him by his last name.

"Wait a minute," I said. "You said he was suffering from a fist fight like me?"

"That's right. His parents were complaining about that this morning. You mean you don't know anything about that?"

Paul must have gotten to him last night, and she thinks that it was just between him and me.

"Oh, yeah, I remember now. I thought I got the worst of our meeting."

"Of course you know that fighting with the campers is a violation of the rules. Would you like to tell me about it?"

"There really isn't anything to say about it," I said, trying to figure out a fast story in my head. "We just didn't get along."

"People don't inflict injury upon one another because they don't get along. I shall get to the bottom of this," she stated as she got up to leave. "You stay in bed and do what the doctor tells you." As she stopped by the door she said, "I don't understand. He is so much bigger than you."

"I'm stronger than I look," I answered in a hurry.

When they were finished with the breakfast dishes, the guys came up to see me. Paul's jaw was discolored, and they all were in a good mood.

"Okay," I said, "tell me all about it."

Paul wouldn't say anything, but Clock was more than happy to fill me in on everything.

"Well, after we left you, we went looking for them. We finally found them drinking down at the boathouse. I guess that is their spot to hang out and drink. They stopped having a good time when we walked in. Lats told them that this was between Naomi's brother and Paul. But Ed and I said that if any of them wanted to join in, we would be happy to accommodate them. Would you believe that none of them volunteered?"

"Boy, you should have seen Paul!" Ed said, "He beat the hell out of that bastard."

"Oh, come on, he was drunk. Even Kuni could have taken him then," Paul stated.

"When the hell is someone going to tell me what happened?" I yelled.

"Well," Clock went on, "Paul didn't say too much, he just told him to stand up. When he did, Paul busted him right in the mouth. He got up a lot slower that time. That guy hit Paul once, but that was the last punch he got. Paul went in under the next punch and rammed him up to the wall. It just took four punches to finish him. Paul hit him twice in the stomach and two in the face. He never got up after that."

"I wish I could have been there to see that," I said. I then told them of my visit from Mrs. Winderberg and how she thought I was the one who fought with him. We had a big laugh when I told them how I told her I was stronger than I look.

"Has anyone seen Naomi? I need to know if she is ok," I asked. No one had seen her at breakfast, so I asked Clock to see if Jean would see if she was okay.

Each one of the guys filled me in on more details of last night. I was surprised that Lats went along with them, but I should have realized that he would come through when we counted on him.

I told Paul not to say anything to Mrs. Winderberg. We could let her go on thinking what she wants and that way only I would get fired.

The rest of the morning was spent with the doctor checking me out and me trying to convince him to let me go back to the shack. I kept waiting for Naomi to sneak by. I wanted to see her and tell her I was sorry for getting her in trouble. I was hoping that they would blame me for all this and since she was a camper they wouldn't say too much to her.

After I finished eating lunch, the nurse came and took the tray away. I wish I wouldn't be so embarrassed when she comes in. For some reason she was extra nice to me this afternoon. She was even calling me Phil. Maybe she felt sorry for me.

It was lunchtime for everyone else, so I just sat in the chair and looked out the window. There was a knock on the door, and thinking it might be Naomi, I hurried over and opened the door. I was a little surprised to see Jean at the door instead.

"How are you feeling, Kuni?" she asked.

"I'm doing okay, I guess. Is Naomi okay?"

"Yeah, she's fine," Jean answered, after hesitating for a moment.

"What's wrong, Jean? Where's Naomi? I need to see her. I need to tell her I'm sorry. She has to forgive me."

"Phil, I'm sorry, but Naomi's parents took her brother and her home."

"What?" I sat up. "What do you mean 'took her home'? Do you mean for good?"

"Yes. She left with her parents about an hour ago. Phil, she wanted to see you, but her father wouldn't let her. She cried and begged him, but he stayed right with her till they left. Her mother kept him outside long enough for her to write you this note," she said as she handed it to me.

I just held on to it for a while, not really believing all this was happening.

"Phil, I'm so sorry you were hurt because of me," the note started. "I should have known something like this would happen, but I was so selfish. All I could see was the happiness you were giving me. I don't have much time and it would take forever to tell you how much you mean to me. Here is an address of a good friend of mine. Please send her your address and I will write a longer letter. [Rebecca Mayer, 15321 W. Division St. Philadelphia Penna.].

"Phil, please, please don't be angry with me for what my brother did. I am so lost and mixed up. I need to know you love me even if we have to be apart. When I came to camp, I was so miserable. I felt so guilty and sad about my abortion; I would lie awake nights and wonder what my baby would have been like. At times I didn't know how I could go on as I laid there and cried. It seemed that everything good had gone out of my life. And then you showed up and brought a smile to my face and made me laugh. Soon I started having feelings I thought had died with everything else. Almost like a prayer you came into my life at a time when I needed you the most. My dearest Philip, I will love you forever for that."

I turned to look out the window, for my eyes were watering and I didn't want Jean to see the tears that were going to come out.

"Phil," Jean came over and put a hand on my shoulder, "I feel so sorry for both of you."

After a few minutes I heard the door close as Jean left. It seemed like hours that I sat there wanting to yell out, to scream how unfair it was, but I just sat there.

Later on Mrs. Winderberg stopped by. As soon as I saw her, I knew she was there to fire me, but by then I just didn't give a damn. I had no reason to still be here.

"May I sit down, Philip?" she said as she sat down on the chair next to the window. "Stairs become more of an obstacle when you become my age. I should have requested that you be put on the ground floor. The doctor informed me that you are in fine health except for some soreness and an assortment of aches and pains. He also explained his desire to keep you here for one more night because of your concussion. I might add, over your strong disagreement."

She paused to give me some time to answer, but hell, I didn't know what to say, so I just kept quiet.

After a while, she went on, "Philip, I am very angry and disappointed with you. I heard all about the infatuation between Naomi and you. This was a rule issued at the beginning of camp and you have violated it. Mr. Pitman insists that you be fired immediately and I quite agree with him. Before coming up here, I held a meeting with the remaining boys to inform them of this decision. But, Paul stated, to my shock, that since everyone started together, they would quit

174

together. It seems that your friends all agree to leave with you if I fire you. Since I cannot have this happen this close to the end of camp, I agreed to allow you to stay on till the end of camp. I'm afraid no one will be allowed to come back next year. Do you have anything to say on your behalf?" she asked, after pausing for a moment.

"No, I don't," I answered, "I'm sorry I caused so much trouble for everyone, I never meant to. Most of all I am sorry that I hurt Naomi. Please don't blame the rest of the guys. This was all my fault."

She sat there for about a minute before she spoke again, "Philip, I am sad to let you boys go. All of you were very nice children and I don't think I will find better workers. Although there would be something to say for the loyalty and companionship between you boys, I cannot allow ultimatums to be issued or rules to be broken. The rule was created to prevent such an incident like this from happening. A relationship like this is wrong because you are both from different worlds."

Mrs. Winderberg got up to leave. "You may have the rest of the week to rest up, Philip, but I will need to have you start again this weekend. Would that be agreeable to you?"

"I feel fine, Mrs. Winderberg. I could start tomorrow."

"No, Philip, let's do what the doctor suggested."

Mrs. Winderberg walked to the door and turned to face me. "I happen to be good friends with Mrs. Pitman and I know the circumstances involved with Naomi coming up to camp this summer. I also know how Mr. Pitman dominates Mrs. Pitman and Naomi. I'm afraid this incident only made matters worse. I understand the pain and sadness you kids are going through now, but it is just part of growing, and it will pass."

"Mrs, Winderberg," I said, as she started to turn to go, "when we were together we were happy. The pain and sadness came when they broke us apart. What part of the relationship would you say was wrong?"

She stood there for a minute and then left without answering.

I went back to the shack the next morning, and for the rest of the week, I just moped around. We went into town and I found an old record of "As Time Goes By." Using the cook's record player, I spent most of the days listening to that and just feeling sorry for the both of us. I would daydream of driving up to her house and rescuing her from her parents. Then we would drive off together and be together for the rest of our lives. Deep down I knew I probably would never see her again. But I think I would always see her sitting by the piano in the gym or running down the hill to meet me. I would remember how we hid in the back of Paul's truck, hanging on to one another. I would remember that night in the field, the tenderness and love we shared as we laid under the blanket. The sadness I felt now and the joy of the memories were swimming around in my head, and I didn't know what to feel. This was the first time I felt so mixed up. I was glad when I was able to start back to work Saturday morning.

the wine with. About the only thing we could come up with were some water glasses.

"Hey, let's have a toast," I said when Ed poured wine for all of us.

"Lats should give it," Ed said, "since it was all his idea."

"It was not my idea. I didn't say anything about this."

"Lats, they're on a roll now, so just say a toast," Paul said.

"Okay," Lats went on, "here's to a great summer. I had a good time this summer."

And down we drank. I think every one of us gave a shudder after that first drink. That first glass went down hard. *Boy, that was lousy*, I thought.

Clock said as he wiped off his mouth, "Boy, that was good."

"Yeah, it sure was," I lied as everyone else agreed. Ed wanted another drink.

"I wish there was some way we could have cooled it," Paul said. "It's as warm as piss."

"How do you know how warm that is?" Clock asked.

"He can tell when it runs down his leg," I replied.

We all laughed and snickered at our joke, Ed filled up the glasses for another round. Lats and Paul decided that was enough for them. It looked like the wine was getting Lats sick, and Paul claimed he had to stay sober so he could take care of us when we got drunk.

"Drunk! What do you mean, get drunk?" I said, "We can handle wine; it's just grapes. Right?"

"Ed and I wouldn't get drunk, but I bet Kuni does," Clock stated.

"Let's have another drink," Ed kept saying.

I must have been wrong before. After the third glass, this wine didn't taste bad at all.

"Clock, remember the time we got Horse drunk on that hard cider?" I asked.

"Yeah, I sure do," Clock answered as he started to laugh hard about that.

With Clock and I both laughing, it must have been contagious as the rest of them were starting to laugh a little.

"Well, tell us about it," Paul demanded.

"One night Tom, Kuda, Clock, and I got a hold of some hard cider. We decided to get Horse drunk. I don't think he ever drank before. We asked Horse if he wanted to go up to the Sugar Bowl in Forest City with us. On the way up we passed this jug of hard cider around, but we just pretended to drink out of it. Horse was the only one to really drink it. He kept asking us if it was empty yet. By the time we got up to the Sugar Bowl, Horse had drunk most of the bottle.

Clock said, "Yeah, remember when he thought that parking meter in Forest City was his girlfriend, and he was so drunk he was kissing it?"

"His girl friend never was very good looking," I added. We all laughed about that.

"Hey, let's have another drink," Ed said.

We continued to reminisce about the good old days, and that's not easy to do because when you are only sixteen, the good old days happened last month. Most of the cheese was gone by now, and we were on our second gallon.

With our drinks, we sat on the bunks talking and laughing. Most anything we said seemed funny now. As I looked at Ed, I noticed that he was leaning over. At first I didn't know if it was Ed or me. But then he kept leaning over till he fell off the bunk. Paul went over and picked Ed up.

"I told you guys you were going to get drunk."

"Drunk hell, Paul," Ed said. "I was just checking something out on the floor."

"It wasn't his fault, Paul. I've been noticing things move also. It's spooky the way the stuff in here keeps moving," I stated as I stood up and had to hold on to the wall.

"Both of you are drunk," Paul said in disgust.

"I'll drink to that. Let's have another," Clock replied.

"Oh, no! Not you, too," Paul said as he went back to his bunk.

I got up and staggered over to Paul and asked for the wine.

"I'm not Paul. I'm Lats."

I got close to get a better look, as things were getting a little foggy. "By damn, you are Lats. What the hell are you doing looking like Paul?"

Clock, Ed and I filled our glasses again and that killed the second gallon.

Ed was trying to say something to Lats and Paul, but they couldn't understand him. I don't see why they didn't, he sounded normal to me.

"You had to open your big mouth," Paul said to Lats. "See, all three of them are drunk now."

"Oh go to hell, Paul," Lats replied.

"I don't know about you guys, but I'm going," Clock said. He then drank down the last of his wine and stood up to leave. "Whoa!" he said as he fell back on the bed.

"Are you ok?" Paul asked.

"Sure, nothing to it," Clock answered as he got up a lot slower this time. "The wine doesn't have any effect on me! I can drink another gallon, and it wouldn't bother me at all."

Starting towards the door he proceeded to hit his head on the light bulb. Holding on to his head, he then walked into the door. "I'm okay! I'm okay!" he said while the light kept swinging back and forth.

"Where are you going?" I asked.

"Up to the canteen."

"Hey, that's a good idea," Ed said. "Let's all go."

"Boy, you guys are drunk," Paul stated.

"Drunk hell, Paul, this stuff hasn't affected me yet," I said as I leaned forward to balance myself.

"I'm not Paul and stop breathing in my face," Lats said.

"Oh, sorry." I turned and said, "Drunk hell, Paul, this stuff…"

"I'm Ed."

"Oh sorry, Ed. Well, where the hell are you, Paul?"

"Over here," he answered.

I strained to see his face and walked over to him. I kept my eyes on his face so I wouldn't lose him again. I walked right into his face.

Paul fell back, yelling, "He broke my nose, he broke my nose!" as he held his nose, rolling around on his bed.

We finally got Paul settled down so Lats could stop his nose from bleeding. Paul calmed down a lot when he decided that his nose was okay.

"You had to open your big mouth, Lats."

After that we headed up to the canteen. Lats said he would not have anything to do with a bunch of drunken bums like us, but he and Paul came along anyway to keep us out of trouble.

On the way up, I couldn't understand how the path could have gotten so narrow. I kept walking into the hedges. Things didn't get any better at the canteen. I walked down those stairs real good. It wasn't my fault that I missed the last one.

Paul helped me up and led me to a booth but he had to leave me there to go help Lats. It seemed that Clock had managed to climb on top of a table and was trying to give a speech. Lats and Paul were trying to help him down, but he managed to fall on top of a girl anyway.

Two girls had Ed over in the corner, and he was telling them a dirty joke. After a while Clock and I were finally settled down in our booth. Paul had Lats stand guard while he went to get Ed. It seems that one of the girls didn't want to hear the punch line of Ed's joke, and Ed was chasing her around the canteen trying to tell it to her.

Eventually, Paul managed to get us all together. We had a hard time trying to keep Clock down; he was trying to climb over to the next booth to talk to girls there. I never did see how he did it, but Ed was dancing a slow dance with that same girl he was chasing earlier. She yelled something at him and slapped his face. Ed came staggering back to the booth.

"Do you think I left something out?" he asked.

Just about that time, Paul decided we had enough and started us out of there. I tried to make those stupid stairs again but the higher I brought my feet, the higher the step got. I finally fell on my face. I pulled myself up using the nearest pretty leg I could see. Paul again had to come to my rescue because the dumb girl was beating me over the head with her purse.

"Let go of her leg, you idiot!" Paul yelled at me.

Some old man was helping me up and asked Paul what kind of wine I drank.

"Drink? No, he's too young to drink," Paul said.

"Boy, did we drink. I would invite you down for a drink but we finished it all."

"You better take him back to his bed before my wife sees him," the man replied.

"So he doesn't want to drink with us. Who the hell does he think he is?"

"He's the boss, you dope," Paul answered.

"Oh."

On the way back we went through the baseball field and there were couples all over the place yelling at us to shut up and get out of there.

"Paul," I said. "Are we going to let them get away with calling us all those names?"

"No, Paul, don't listen to him. He's drunk," Lats pleaded.

"Paul, I think one of them just said something nasty about your girlfriend."

"Paul, don't listen to Kuni."

"Well, Paul?"

"Hell, no, Kuni, I'm not going to let them get away with that," he answered. "Let's go."

We all climbed on the back of Sherman II, and Paul started it up. We drove onto the field to say 'hello' to all of them. As Paul drove around with the lights on bright, we were jumping up and down screaming in the back of the truck. By their reactions I don't think they were a bit friendly to us, not one of them had a nice word to say to us. There were some girls that should have thanked us, and one couple who were too late to thank us. With the lights hitting the couples, all we saw was the girls trying to button up and the guys grabbing up the blankets and cursing us. We cleared that field off in a hurry. Maybe they would thank us in the morning, or maybe not.

CAMP LAURA

We finally got back to the shack and the first thing Ed did was to visit the swamp in the back of the shack.

After listening to Ed barf for a while I decided to go back there and join him. Paul followed me back to make sure we didn't drown. I brought a chair with me and sat down in the swamp and proceeded to barf my guts out.

Ed was laying face down in the swamp, sick all over himself. "Ed, look at yourself getting sick like that. You shouldn't drink until you can handle it like the rest of us," I said during a pause between barfs.

"What the hell are you squeaking about? You're doing the same thing," Paul yelled at me.

I thought about that for a while and said, "Yeah, but at least I'm sitting down."

"Christ, I don't know why I bother."

"Paul," Lats called out. "You better help me with Clock. He's running up and down the road with just his shorts on."

"For Christ's sake."

Paul and Lats went chasing after Clock. A couple of cars stopped and watched as those two were dragging Clock back in the shack.

"Kuni, where did Ed go?" Paul asked as they tried to settle Clock down.

"I don't know. He took a bar of soap and left," I answered.

"Lats, this is all your fault," Paul said as he took off for the showers, with the rest of us following.

Ed was standing under the shower, sopping wet and all soaped up.

"Ed, why the hell didn't you take your clothes off?" Paul asked.

"Oh," Ed said as he looked down at his wet clothes covered with soap. "How about that?"

We helped Paul get Ed back to the shack. Trying to climb into his bunk, he passed out half way there.

"The hell with it. Let him sleep that way."

I lay down on my bunk and promptly fell off. "This damn bed is floating."

"You're crazy," Clock said. "The whole shack is floating away in the swamp."

I put both feet on the floor and that slowed it down some. The last thing I remember was Clock telling Paul how lucky Ed and I were that Clock was sober enough to take care of us.

I awoke the next morning with Paul shaking the bunk telling me it was time to get up. I wish he wouldn't scream it out so loud. The first thing I saw was Clock sitting up in his bunk sound asleep. I threw my feet on the floor and jumped up. What a stupid move that was. I groaned and slowly set myself back down. I just realized that my head was too large and heavy for the rest of my body to hold it up. If I move again it would roll off my neck.

"Paul, am I dead?" I asked.

"You're not that lucky," he answered.

I pleaded with Paul to get me a bucket of water. When he did, I lowered myself to the floor and crawled outside. I stuck my head in the bucket of water and left it there until I felt a flicker of life somewhere in my body. Sitting up, I saw Paul grinning.

"Go to hell, Paul. What's with Clock?" I mumbled softly as he was still asleep sitting up.

"Nothing, he fell asleep like that. He wouldn't shut up; he kept me awake half the night. He stopped in the middle of a sentence and when I looked over at him, he was sound asleep."

Ed was just lying there staring at the ceiling, so Paul asked him if he was going to get up.

"I think I pissed my pants. They're all wet."

Paul looked at me and we both grinned.

"Yeah Ed, you must have pissed your pants while you were sleeping," Paul answered.

"How come my shirt and pillow are all wet?"

"Well Ed, you drank a lot of wine last night."

"Oh shit, don't tell anyone about this, ok?"

"Ed, you have to know that this is going in the yearbook. Come on over and you can share my bucket."

"Thanks." Ed crawled over to me. He made it halfway before he got sick again. Paul and I helped him outside and sat him up against the shack while he got over the dry heaves.

Paul woke Clock up, and he jumped out of bed. He grabbed a towel, took a shower, and came back whistling.

"I hate you," I told him.

"Where's Lats?" Clock asked Paul.

"He already left. He said he didn't want to have anything to do with you drunks."

"I hate him, too," I said. I figured a shower would make me feel somewhat human again. It didn't.

We went up to the kitchen and got our breakfast trays. No sooner had Ed put his tray down that he got up and ran out. I wasn't too far behind him. When we got back, Clock was finished with his breakfast and eating some of ours.

"I really do hate you, Clock," I said.

Three days later when we were getting ready to leave, my stomach was still a little shaky.

Packing our stuff into the back of Sherman, we were all a little sad to be leaving. Summer was coming to an end and pretty soon we would be starting our senior year. I had wanted so badly to say goodbye to Naomi, to see her face again, to hold her in my arms again, to kiss her tears away. We all went back to the shack for one last look around and walked back to the truck.

"Wait a minute," I said as I went back and took down our "Stalag 17" sign. With the sign under my arm, I took one last look around and ran to catch up with the rest of the guys.

CHAPTER TWENTY-TWO

It's hard to believe that so many years have passed since that summer. I don't know how often my wife has asked me why I keep that old sign. I probably should have thrown it away years ago. I wonder if any of the old gang would remember it.

After graduation the old gang pretty much went different ways. We were such good friends, but time has a way of diminishing even that.

Lats had a bunch of scholarships after we graduated, and he went on to college. He made out pretty good for a small town boy. The last time I heard of him, he was a mining engineer. There for a while we all thought he would marry Alice. They went together for a while, but it fizzled out. He moved out to the western part of Pennsylvania somewhere.

Paul married his childhood sweetheart in his senior year, and after graduation they moved to Philadelphia. I guess he got tired of taking care of us kids and decided to have some of his own. After he moved, we lost track of him completely.

I went into the Army right after graduation, with Clock and Ed following about a month later. Although I had never met up with Clock and Ed in the service, we did get together when we got out. After bumming around for a while, Ed met a really nice girl and got married. He moved to the town next to ours and settled down. I saw him whenever I went back to visit my parents. Ed's bad health finally caught up to him, and he passed away about three years ago.

Clock and I moved to New York City where we continued our crazy ways for a while. We both got married with Clock and his wife moving up to New England, and I headed out west. He did make it to college and became a high school history teacher.

Right after that summer Naomi and I started writing to each other through her friend. At first the letters were regular, but as our senior year went on, the letters became intermittent. I was in basic training at Fort Dix when we wrote and set up a meeting. I had a weekend furlough coming, and we agreed to meet at a shopping mall. I saw her sitting at a table with a couple of her girlfriends. She spotted me right away because I was in uniform. After she introduced me to her friends, she pulled me away.

"Let's go sit at another table." Naomi said.

"God, it's great seeing you again." I said. And it was, she was still beautiful, but she seemed older and sadder. We talked a while about that summer and filled each other in on our life since then. It was time to go, and I realized everything had changed. This would be the last time I would see her. We said our goodbyes and started to walk away, when she turned and ran back to me, hugged and kissed me.

"Phil, that summer will always be the best time of my life. I will never forget it, and I will always love you for it," she said, and as her eyes teared up, she turned and walked away.

When I went overseas we wrote a few times and then it stopped. I thought of her a lot when I would try to go to sleep on my cot. I had wanted to write to her again to tell her I was having a hard time forgetting her and maybe I didn't want to.

One night I decided to write to her again to see how she was. This time a letter came back from her friend.

She wrote to say she was sorry to tell me that Naomi had died. One night she had filled the bathtub with hot water and lay down in the tub and slit her wrist.

I stayed in the barracks that night when everyone else went out. I lay on my bunk thinking that if she were with me, she would still be alive now. If only I could have been there to hold her, maybe she wouldn't have done it. She had once told me that when I held on to her, that my heart spoke to her heart. God, I wish she could hear it now. That night for the last time in my life I cried.

"Dad, we're ready to go home now." Kim said.

We walked up to the car, and while the kids got in, I turned for one last look around.

"What are you waiting on, Dad?" Mike asked.

"I'll be right there Mike, I'm just saying goodbye to some old friends."

Made in the USA
Monee, IL
27 August 2023

41725399R00108